To Gwen

umpivteel

WHEN THE BOUGH BREAKS

BREAKS

By Linda Fewtrell

ONE

She lay on the filthy, lumpy shakedown bed in the corner of the dark and dingy room, too young to be going through the pains of labour that would bring another mouth to feed. She closed her eyes against the pain, terrified of the ordeal ahead of her. Watching her mother go through the same torment year after year did not ease her fear or her pain. Fighting back the tears so that she did not frighten her younger siblings, she rocked back and forth and cursed her father for forcing this on her.

He had started to paw at her when after her fourteenth birthday, kissing her full on her mouth with his pungent breath turning her stomach. Resistance had only led to slaps and punches until poor Alice was barely conscious when he had raped her. It happened at least weekly when he came staggering home smelling of alcohol and stale smoke. He had stopped bothering his sad shell of a wife once he saw his daughters' pert breasts developing. 'The mad bitch is no good to anyone now and I need what I need,' he had muttered often enough to himself to justify his lusting for his daughter.

Alice had become frightened for her younger sisters in case their dad started on them. Sally, her younger sister worked at the Manor house laundry and was well out of it. She had been reluctant to leave her family at such a young age and did not understand Alice's reasons for pushing her to leave. Sally with r startling blue eyes, a bonnie round face and golden hair would grow to be a stunner. Her body was already beginning to develop at twelve and it was inevitable that her father would soon start pawing at the young lass.

Cissy was only eight and so still too small for her brutish father, but he would turn on her as soon as her body began to develop. So, Alice bit her lip and laid still through the torture, always planning to escape somehow but knowing she couldn't. Who else would look after her sick mother and the babies?

Another contraction hit and Alice moaned aloud, her mother sat by the empty fire grate staring at the floor completely oblivious to her surroundings. The small child who lay on the bed near her started crying when startled from sleep. The pain subsided, and she gently pulled herself up to look at little Harry. The poor mite was so small for his age and had a sickly pallor.

'Cissy, Bring him over here will yer?' The child struggled to pick up the whimpering toddler and half carried, and half dragged him over to where her sister sat slumped against the support of the wall, then she unceremoniously dumped him onto the grubby mattress by Alice's side. The Jolt made him cry out with a loud wail, but the child's mother sat by the meagre fire and gazed down at the floor unaware of the infant's needs. She began to hum a lullaby quietly, her head hung low and nodding slightly in rhythm. Her fingers worked at the threadbare shawl around her shoulder tugging at the loose threads. She would occasionally glance aimlessly around the dim room with no flowers, only darkness, dirt, and hungry forlorn faces. She would turn her head back to the floor and disappear back into her warm safe world.

Alice rocked the crying child gently and asked Cissy to fetch the bag of pap for the boy to suckle on. This mix of flour and watery milk would be enough to quieten him but has no real food value. She had made a thin mutton stew out in the little scullery but only enough to feed their dad.

'You look bad our Alice, should I go and get Kitty?'

'No, I don't need her yet. I'll be okay in a minute. Take our Dolly over to Tess Harvey, she said she would watch for you and Dolly when my time came.' She puffed air through her lips and ran her arm across her forehead and then added. 'Keep an eye open for Eddie and George as well, she said she would see to them if they were about. Tess is a good sort.'

'What about our mam?' Cissy asked with a glance in her mother's direction.

'Don't worry about her Cissy, she doesn't even know what day it is.' Alice snapped back at her sister. It was so difficult to keep her temper with things the way they were. The pains were getting worse and closer together.

Daily life became harder to bear as the pregnancy sucked the life force from her. With no time to learn and play Alice's childhood had been brief. At three years old, she fetched and carried for her mother and her younger siblings that came yearly. She could not remember all the various places they had lived, but this one was worse.

Cissy pulled at her young sister, who until she had heard her name mentioned had been playing happily with a stick in the earth floor where she had wet. She had needed to 'go' for ages but was too afraid to ask either of her sisters while the atmosphere was so tense. So had wet where she sat and played happily in the resulting mud. Dolly was nearing her third birthday but still unsteady on her feet, due to being born with a crooked foot that turned outwards at the toes. She always went barefoot; ill-fitting old shoes caused her too much pain.

'Come on Dolly'. Cissy urged her sister to her feet with a rough tug. She had no patience for her siblings and pushed them around carelessly.

Once the girls had left Alice fell back on the lumpy mattress giving in to the wave of pain creeping up her back and around her stomach. She prayed she would have the strength to feed the little mite with her milk. For months she had sacrificed her share of the meagre meals so that the younger ones could eat. Her mother ate little, especially when dad sat near her, but would help herself in the night to any scraps Alice managed to put aside for her.

Alice's small, childish body looked grotesque with the swollen belly protruding out in front like a potato in the middle of a sock. It had become impossible to hide her shame with her ragged shawl so Cissy and the boys would go down to the market most days for her. They had become quite adept at begging for the spoilt veggies and often came home with more than they had the money for.

She rested between pains until darkness fell.

Cissy burst through the door with her usual boisterousness and called out loudly, breaking the silence and startling the occupants of the room, including her mother who cowered at the sudden noise.

'Mrs Harvey sent me to see if you are all right.' She stopped dead in her tracks when she saw her sister's pale, drawn face. Her baby brother stirred and opened his eyes. 'Should I take him back with me?' she asked in a much quieter tone. Alice simply nodded her reply. 'I'm going to send for old Kitty one of the boys can go.' Cissy carried Harry out of the room and over to Tess Harvey's house. Alice did not object.

* * *

A loud knock on the door announced the arrival of a large elderly woman, she flounced through the door filling the room with her enormous body and presence.

'Yer times on yer Eh, Let us 'ave a look an' see how much longer yer gonna be then.' Old Kitty crossed the room to where Alice lay, throwing a large cloth bag on the table as she hobbled on her arthritic legs. 'Still feeling sorry for yourself then Nell?' The old woman uttered a loud 'TUT' when the sad figure did not acknowledge Kitty's presence. Alice moaned with the pain and drew Kitty back to the job she was here to do. She crouched down and with a grunt fell to her knees. 'Couldn't get to the bed

5

then? Suppose that miserable old sod would have summit to say about it. Eh?' She never expected an answer. 'Right then.' She exclaimed as she threw the girl's skirt over her swollen stomach and pulled the skinny legs apart. Plunging her dirty hand into Alice's groin and then withdrawing it after a quick examination, Kitty said 'Got ages yet' she pulled the skirt back down and stood up, 'Just go with the pain girl and let me know when the urge to push takes yer.'

Old Kitty hobbled back over to the well-scrubbed wooden table, rubbing her knees as she protested. 'Bloody arfritis, not so good on me pins as I used to be. Never mind I have me own medication.' She reached into the ragged cloth bag she had tossed onto the table and pulled out a brown bottle. 'Want some Nell?' She offered the gin bottle. 'Nah! Yer never did take a drink. I fink yer would 'ave bin better off if yer 'ad. The odd drop of gin got me through. Buried two 'husbands I 'ave, and four of me kids. You don't see me feeling sorry for mesel do yer?'

She sat herself down on a rickety chair and continued to relate her life history to her captive audience until the gin took hold and she dozed off with her head on the table and her hands dangling down by her side. The empty gin bottle hit the floor with a thud. She lay quite still with saliva drooling from her mouth breaking the silence occasionally with a snort.

Alice's pains grew stronger, and she felt the need to push, she pleaded with God to get her through this. Her cries woke Kitty with a start and for a while she forgot where she was, rubbing her eyes and stretching her arms wide she took in her surroundings. Still half asleep she stumbled across to where Alice lay. Cissy burst through the door.

'How's our Alice?'

'Get yersel over 'ere Cissy and give us an 'and.' The old woman knelt by Alice. 'Fill that bowl over there with hot water and find some cloth or towels. Mind yer doesn't scald yersel.' Cissy's timing was perfect. She quickly busied herself as a midwife's assistant.

Amid the chaos, Nell sat watching the scene quietly

smiling about nothing.

A small, wiry man walked uneasily into the room, scowling. Albert Allerton's shift on the docks had finished hours ago, but a payday meant he could spend time and money with his mates. Through bleary, bloodshot eyes he tried to focus on the shadowy figures on the floor. Staggering further into the room, worse for his visit to the alehouse, he slurred.

'Don't bother with me tea I've had a pie down in the 'Dog 'n gun.' He peered through the gloom and saw his eldest daughter lying on her back with her knees up and her lower body exposed. Her long, dark, mattered hair hung limply on the makeshift pillow of an old coat rolled into a sausage that Cissy had shoved under her head. The old hag the locals called a midwife crouched on the floor with her head between Alice's knees. His other daughter Cissy busied herself pouring hot water from an exceptionally large kettle into a bowl on the floor close to the old woman's knees. He quickly turned and looked away, as he moved towards the bedroom door he bellowed, 'God, get me out of here.' he slammed the bedroom door behind him.

Once on the other side of the door, he threw himself on the bed, through the alcohol-induced fog he suddenly made sense of the scene he had seen.

'Bleedin ell,' he thought, 'another soddin mouth to feed.' He had no regrets over his use of Alice, his wife had been less than useless after that last kid had been born dead. She refused to speak. She just sat there every day by the fireplace only moving to visit the 'lav'. The stupid woman wouldn't come to bed, she screamed if he went near her. It wasn't the screaming that bothered him so much as the extra effort it took to get his rights. 'No, he consoled himself. Alice teased him, wearing her skirts above her ankles, and good to look at too. Why waste good money on a whore when a young lass sat available at home.' He reasoned if he hadn't taken her some other bloke would. He had done her a favour, showing her what life would be. 'Fancy her get herself stuck with a kid though, silly cow. Just like her bloody mother, no sooner do I 'ang me trousers up she fell for

7

another kid.' He muttered away to himself until he fell into a drunken sleep.

Back in the other room Alice gave one final scream and pushed a small squirming red-faced baby into the world. Kitty cut the cord and handed the wet bundle to Alice.

'It's a girl.' She said matter-of-factly and turned her attention back to the afterbirth. Alice gently held her tiny daughter, looking down at her red face screwed up in anger, her eyes tightly shut and her mouth opened with a whimper. She resembled little Dolly when she had been born, with the same wispy hair and button nose.

She thought of the life waiting for this one and her heart filled with dread.

Kitty and Cissy busied themselves clearing up the mess the best they could, it wasn't a job for an eight-year-old, the old woman knew that, but she couldn't do it on her own and Nell wasn't up to it.

'Right,' Kitty exclaimed, 'That's my bit done.' She slowly got to her feet and brushed down her skirt, she reached out for the gin bottle, but it was not where she had left it. Her foot kicked the empty bottle, and it rolled towards Nell. 'Did you take a sneaky sip of my medicine you sod? I was saving that.' She shrugged and shook her head as she retrieved the bottle and then shoved it back into the bag. Meanwhile, Alice took a small bag of copper coins she had hidden under the mattress and handed them to Kitty.

'Thanks, Kitty.' She said as she held the coins out. Kitty took the bag and counted the coppers. She normally charged more. After studying and counting them again, she looked around the room and down at the sleeping baby then as an act of compassion she handed the coppers back to Alice.

'Here, you need them more.'

Alice protested with a shake of her head

'No, I must pay,' her eyes wide in surprise at the old woman's gesture.

'Don't be daft lass.' Kitty forced the bag into Alice's hand.

She pointed towards the closed bedroom door, and, with a nod of her head, she said. 'It's well-known around 'ere who did this.' She bent her head closer to Alice. 'Do yersel favour and get out of 'ere and take Cissy with yer cos' she'll be next.'

Alice watched speechless as the old woman gathered her belongings into the cloth bag, all of which had fallen from the threadbare bag as she rooted for the gin bottle. Waddling across the room on her arthritic legs Kitty turned and looked at Nell, tutted and shook her head before leaving.

The old woman left, and Alice cried. With floods of tears, she cried and wailed, releasing the pain and terror she had endured over the years. The fears for her younger sisters and the humiliation suffered at her father's hands, all this she had endured without tears. Yet some, well-meant words, and a kind act from that old woman broke down the wall of denial she had built to protect her sanity and prevent her from becoming her mother. The kind act from Kitty in refusing her rightful payment and showing a little pity was too much to bear.

Cissy could do nothing but stand and stare at her sister in amazement. She had never seen Alice cry, not even when David and Sophie died of fever two years ago. Cissy could not fathom the need for her sister to cry so hard, the pain was supposed to be over. When the baby also started to cry Nell moaned loudly covering her ears with her hands and rocking on the stool like a child, trying to cut out the real world.

'Hush Alice, please hush.' She patted her sister's back the way Alice had done when she had fallen and badly scraped her knee. She hummed gently as if quietening the babies, there were no words to lullabies, there had been no one to teach them.

'For pity's sake stop that infernal row,' Bert screamed at anyone who might heed him. 'Can't a working man get any peace?'. Alice was shocked into silence. He stood in the bedroom doorway partially clothed in a dirty torn vest and stained underwear. When peace descended, he returned to the bedroom slamming the door behind him.

Cissy rhythmically patted her sister's back, quietly

shushing the sobbing girl while Nell curled up into a tight ball making herself small and invisible.

'It'll be all right our Alice, 'onest. I'll help more, I will!' she nodded to assure her. 'And Mam will come around soon, I'm sure she will.' Alice continued to sob, and the baby cried louder. 'Look feed yer baby, that'll help.' Alice looked down at the crying red-faced infant covered in body fluids from its birth. She gently stroked the warm cheeks and the little mouth searched for food. Alice parted her blouse and gave her baby her breast, at once the baby stopped crying and suckled. 'There,' Cissy said quietly, 'I told yer it would be all right.' Quietly pleased with herself for taking charge as an adult.

'Yes.' Alice sobbed 'It'll be all right, I'm sure.' As the infant suckled at her breast the new mother prayed her life could surely not get any worse.

TWO

Tess Harvey hated crossing the road to the Allerton's hovel, it always upset her seeing how Cissy lived. The poverty and cruelty she knew existed in that place were unbearable. However, she must find the courage to check the welfare of the sweet child who brought so much light into her heart since her husband William died. She had not seen the children for a while and was becoming increasingly worried. The father went off to work most mornings and staggered home drunk every evening. The two oldest boys, she assumed were still working at the factory. She usually heard them shouting on the street in the early hours, after leaving the other young thugs they hung about with.

She looked around cautiously as she crossed the narrow road, praying that Bert would be out at work or down the pub. She thought him an odious, uncouth, foul-mouthed creature she would rather not have anything to do with. The common knowledge around the neighbourhood of his criminal activities meant that most decent people avoided him.

Timidly she tapped at the rough wooden door. She heard shuffling feet then the door opened. A small, ragged boy with an unwashed face and runny nose smiled at her and said, 'Oh, Hiya Mrs Harvey.' The boy sniffed hard and coughed harshly, rubbing his face into his sleeve adding to the grime with contents from his nose. He looked at her expectantly waiting for her to say why she had come.

'Hello, Eddie.' She spoke softly and bent forward slightly to make herself appear nearer the boy's size. The bulky figure she knew would often frighten little ones. 'I was wondering, could I speak to Cissy?' she asked. At that Alice appeared behind the boy and gently pushed him aside.

'I'm sorry Mrs Harvey, please come in.' Alice stepped back to allow the stout woman to enter.

'Please sit down.' She said as she shooed one of her young brothers off the dining chair so the visitor could sit. As Tess Harvey moved towards the table her eyes adjusted to the dimness.

One small, grimy window looked out into the street, over it hung a heavy, tatty chenille curtain blocking any light that may make its way through the dirty glass to permeate the gloom. The earthen floor looked damp in places and trodden smooth but still uneven so that the well-scrubbed table taking up the centre of the room wobbled. The chair the child had vacated on one side looked sturdy and a rough plank balanced on two wooden packing cases along the other create a bench. The surface of the table showed signs of scrubbing with soap and a scrubbing brush leaving a concaved centre.

On a large mattress in the corner of the small room, small white feet at various angles protruded from under a black blanket like snowdrops peeking through the dark earth.

Alice pushed the unwashed plates and utensils scattered on the table, to one side.

'I expect you are looking for our Cissy,' Alice asked in a dull lifeless tone. 'Were you wanting her to run some errands?'

'No. No,' Tess shook her head. She was still reeling from her first impression of the cramped living quarters these children endured. 'I just wondered if everything was OK as I hadn't seen Cissy for a few days.' Alice understood the older woman's concern. This kind neighbour was very fond of Cissy, giving her treats for running the odd errand.

She cleared a place for Tess Harvey to sit and again asked

her to sit down on the chair.

'Please sit-down Mrs Harvey, I'll brew some tea.' Most people around the street ignored her but Tess Harvey was different, always there lending a helping hand to a troubled neighbour. Mrs Harvey would give hungry children the end of a loaf with a scraping of beef dripping. She was always the first to start a collection of coppers to bury a poor soul with dignity.

At this moment she sat in the Allerton's squalid home to give Alice support in whatever way she could. For the first time since she entered the room, Tess looked at the young girl's thin drawn face. Looking after a large family with no help left Alice about to collapse. The thin cotton dress, patched with so many scraps it no longer had any resemblance to its original fabric, hung off her tiny frame. The child had dark circles under her huge dark eyes. Her skin was as pale as death.

'No Alice, you sit down, I will make the tea. You look worn out.' Alice shook her head her face crumpled with grief, ready to burst into tears.

'I'm sorry.' Her voice was as weary as her body. She sat heavily on the chair she previously offered to her guest. 'I am so tired.' The tears began to fill her eyes.

'You sit there while Auntie Tess mashes the tea.' Tess laid her shawl on the makeshift bench and rolled up her sleeves. She sided the dishes away into a large, chipped bowl and carried them into the tiny scullery. The blackened kettle was full of boiling water ready to pour over the few precious leaves she spooned from the wooden tea caddy.

While she busied herself, Alice remained sitting at the table her head in her hands. The heavy silence was shattered by the dishes clattering together as the heavy middle-aged woman mashed the tea. There was no milk, so she served it black.

'Here you are, lass.' She placed the chipped cup in front of Alice. Slowly Alice lifted her head and smiled at the kind face. Tess sat opposite on the rickety plank. 'Do you want to talk?' She said tenderly to the sad young girl. The dark rings framed her reddened eyes, she looked ten years older than her true age.

Alice shrugged her shoulders and replied.

'There's nowt to say.' She said disparagingly. Tess tapped the back of Alice's hands in a friendly gesture showing empathy with this young girl and her plight. In silence, they drank the weak tea. Tess surveyed the room, the poverty in the house was displayed in every nook and cranny. The child in front of her tried to bring a modicum of comfort to this dreary place. The evidence in the worn faded curtain at the window and withered wildflowers in a precariously placed cracked jar on the fire mantle. The scullery was tidy, the few provisions lined up neatly, the shelves lined with paper once decorative but now yellow with age.

Alice lay her head again on her hand and fell asleep. Tess turned her attention to the other children; they had been unnaturally quiet. She now noticed Cissy sitting quietly on the mattress in the dark corner of the room, two small figures lay near her. The boys Eddie and George sat with their backs against the wall on the other end of the 'bed.' Tess looked again at Cissy, and she saw her bottom lip trembling, and her eyes were filling with tears. With a heavy heart, she stood and went over to Cissy, kneeling in front of the child she took her grubby little hands into her own,

'Come here.' She said pulling the weeping child into the safety of her arms. 'Ah! Lass.' She rocked the small frame and gently stroked the mass of matted hair. Tess had never seen her beloved Cissy in such a state. She was such a strong child, so full of life and optimism. Her confidence and bright personality were the qualities that kept this sweet child forever in the woman's heart. Cissy ran errands for her without a word of complaint. She always had a bright warming smile for others, even though she had lived through the bitter fights and arguments which were a daily occurrence in this house. She constantly thought of ways to help and protect her younger siblings from their brute of a father. She fetched the youngster's small treats given to her by the grateful neighbours who always called on Cissy to run an errand or help on washdays. Now she was a small insecure creature weeping uncontrollably in her friend's embrace.

As Tess rocked and comforted the child, she looked down at the young children who lay so very still on the mattress, the sight of their thin pale legs brought a realisation of the tragedy that had befallen this family.

She leaned across the mattress and with a free hand uncovered the two figures and touched their small faces. The skin was still slightly warm to the touch, but the children had died. Their poor half-starved little bodies lay as if asleep in each other's arms, now at peace and free from the torment of their wretched existence. Covering the tiny forms again with the worn blanket she turned back to Cissy and continued to comfort the grieving child.

Cissy's crying eased and through the sobs, she tried to explain, 'They were coughing the same as me, but they couldn't stop. They were sick Mrs Harvey. Our Alice tried to get them better, she did.' She nodded and shook her head in her sister's defence. 'She got me better, and George's cough has gone now as well.' Tess was shaking her head in amazement, grief, and horror.

'If only I had realised that Cissy's cough could have been Whooping cough.' Tess thought. A sudden thought struck her and frantically she looked around the room for the basket, in harmony with her thoughts the baby cried out, a healthy hungry cry with no sign of a cough. She sighed with relief.

The baby's crying woke Alice who bent down and took her screaming infant from the old washing basket under the table. She bared her breast to the hungry mouth. Tess silently shed tears for the two souls lost, Dolly would have been coming on three and little Harry was only two weeks off his second birthday.

'Why didn't you send for me Alice? I might have been able to help.' Her voice broke with grief. Alice simply shook her head and shrugged her shoulders. Cissy's sobbing had ground to a sniff, she wiped her eyes with the back of her hand and blew her nose on a none-too-clean dress sleeve.

'Dad said it was only a cold and they would be OK. 'E said he had no money for doctors.' Cissy again jumped to her sister's defence. No One would blame Alice, but Cissy knew that in this house Alice got the blame for everything. 'Me, Eddie and George got better.' She looked up at her friend and asked, 'Why didn't they?' The tears began to flow again and Tess Harvey soothed Cissy, which was all she could do in reply.

Nell slipped out of the room.

'She's going to the 'netty' or just a wander,' Cissy shrugged. Tess Harvey raised her eyebrows at this information, she could not remember the last time the woman of this house had been outside. Cissy tugged at Tess Harvey's sleeve and whispered.

'Mam's taken to wandering the streets, sometimes she's gone for ages.' Cissy looked up at the confused and concerned face of her friend. 'Dad says she's gone barmy, but she's not, is she?' her eyes pleading for words of comfort. All Tess could do was shake her head, how could she upset this child anymore, for once agreeing with her father?

Cautiously Tess Stood up, it was no easy task for a woman of her size and age to rise from such a low position.

'Well! There is no denying this lass, you need help.' Taking Cissy by the hand she led her to the table, Alice was still feeding the baby, so she turned to the younger girl. 'Get yourself in the scullery Cissy and wash those few dishes, I'll have a tidy up in here.'

Cissy took the used teacups into the small square scullery. As she disappeared through the door, the big woman walked a few paces to the small boys, so close in age they could be twins. Eddie was the eldest by nine months and ten days, now at six years old, he considered himself grown-up, much too grownup to start crying like a baby. 'George still cried, a lot his opinion. Eddie's jaw was set in a determination not to cry, George sniffed; tears running down his dirty face leaving tell-tale tram lines in the muck as evidence. Rather than towering over the lads, Tess crouched down to their level with a stifled groan.

'Will you two go a message?' Both boys nodded vigorously, and in such unison, an invisible cord could have fastened them together. 'Pop over to old Kitty's house and ask her to call in as soon as she can.' Again, they nodded and then scrambled to their feet and bolted out of the door like two scared rabbits. 'It won't take much to lay these poor mites out.' She thought to herself, 'but it has to be done properly!' She then called Cissy out from the scullery and dispatched her to fetch the doctor. Once alone with Alice and the baby, she sat at the table and waited.

❊ ❊ ❊

The funeral staff carried two small plain wooden coffins out of number eight Victoria Street, standing in the doorway Alice and Cissy watched the cart slowly drive away. The two ragged boys stood by the girls. Alice cradled baby Flo in her arms, and they were all crying silently. Tess Harvey stood nearby watching the young family in their grief. The neighbours stood about, their heads bowed respectfully, although touched by the tragedy each was thankful for their children's health. A large thickset woman, covered in a thick warm shawl to keep out the cold nudged her friend in the ribs and hoarsely whispered,

'No sign of the parents, Eh!' The second woman's face screwed up and tightly pursed lips tutted in agreement.
Another woman in the group leaned towards them and said quite loudly.

'He's in the Dog 'n Gun, and she's turned daft.' All three now shook their heads in unison.

'Shame!' said one.

'Aye!' said another.

'Bloody awful shame' they all agreed. A small older woman walked over to join the group.

'Someone should be going to the bairn's resting place.' Her old croaky voice added her bit to the sad conversation.

'I'd heard the two eldest lads were to walk with the cart?' asked one.

'Both at work.' Two of them said in unison.

'God help 'em all.' The old woman added as they all walked back to their front doors.

The cart left the street on its way to the burial plot, with no mourners to weep by the pauper's grave, and no mark to say where they lay. A rotund middle-aged lady dressed in black ushered the group of young children into the house. Tess Harvey would make sure they all had a warm meal.

THREE

Albert Allerton first came to this town as a youth of fourteen years. he was now nearing his 45th birthday and every hard year showed in his unshaven, weather-worn face. His mass of red wavy hair was thin and almost grey. When in his prime he'd had a short but wiry build; quite good-looking but never considered handsome. His strong white teeth had decayed badly and the few that remained had now turned yellow with nicotine. Working in the docks had kept his frame muscular but too much ale had given him a paunch and he might have been two or three inches taller than five foot five if his legs and back were straight.

At the end of every shift, he would be at the bar of the 'Dog and Gun' alehouse where he would buy pie and peas from the proprietor, or a bowl of mutton stew. Here he sat night after night glowering at those who pushed past to order their drink from the small hatch, grunting the occasional greeting to those who would greet him. He would stay there in the same place until he was either so drunk that his host would serve him no more, or until the alehouse closed. The outcome of his evening was often dependent on the cash in his pocket, this was his life, work, drink then home to sleep.

Running away from his violent father and the miserable farm had been the first adult decision he had made. Port Darlington had given him his independence. He had lodged with the Paterson's in the early days and had married their daughter Elsie when he was seventeen. It was a loveless match that had only come about as the Paterson's pushed them together. When she had succumbed to his charming ways, and he had taken her innocence it was too late, and marriage became 'necessary'. The couple had continued to share the home with her parents. It was well known that the Paterson's doted on their daughter and all they had would be hers one day. Bert knew it would be a tidy sum, so he stayed and played 'happy families', They had two children, Gregory, and Rudolf, and for ten years the marriage plodded.

One day Elsie found out about Nell. Elsie was plain and motherly; she had put on a huge amount of weight after the boys had been born.
Indulged by her parents she ate and ate and became lazy and slovenly. Nell was young and pretty, ten years his junior. She was beautiful with long hair the colour of tar and her eyes huge and dark. Elsie had gone for him with a heavy iron stew pan when she had found out about her husband with this young slip of a girl. A huge fight developed in the Paterson's house and Elsie with her huge frame almost killed Bert. Then Mr Peterson had thrown him out with just the clothes he stood up in and all he could get in an old flour sack.

He would, even now, sit and contemplate his life and the turn of events after he had set up home with Neil. They were happy in the beginning but once the babies began to arrive and money became scarce with each new mouth to feed, the beatings grew in intensity. He didn't want to beat his wife, but somehow it happened, and he was heartily sorry about it. How he ever got to this state of unhappiness was completely beyond his comprehension. Now his wife was so depressed that she was not aware of his existence unless he raised his voice. Then she would cower in the comer like a chastised puppy, head down hugging herself tightly. His children all hated him or were terrified of him, those that were still alive. Except for young Albert his eldest boy, who was much like his father Yes, Bert was proud of Albert. He never told him of course; he couldn't let the lad get the wrong idea.

❋ ❋ ❋

One evening as Bert sat in the bar thinking of his life and his children, his face pulled at each emotion as it passed through his mind, a big stocky chap stood watching him from across the room. He watched Bert's expressive facial gestures with amusement. What is going on in that perverted mind?' The big fellow thought, shaking his head in wonderment.
The huge dockworker walked across to Bert's corner.

'Now me auld Marra!' His voice boomed. 'What yer doin' these days?' Big Geordie had not seen his old workmate for years, not since leaving for Jarrow in a hurry. Bert looked up in surprise at hearing the familiar voice. A big, crooked grin spread over his face in recognition and joy at seeing his old friend standing over him.

'Bloody 'el man!' His grin grew even wider. What the 'el are you doin' 'ere?' Bert almost leapt out of his seat and grabbed the big man by the hand, shaking it so hard Geordie thought his arm would fall off. 'Ee I never thought I'd see you around 'er again after that last bit of bother.' Bert was referring to an illegal fistfight between Big Geordie and a foreign sailor, one of the many that visit the docks. The authorities had broken up the fight and Big Geordie had gone into hiding because he thought that the sailor was dead or dying. The sailor had not died but was sent packing back to his own country, bruised and rueful, swearing his revenge. Bert called across to the bartender to get his friend a drink and the giant from Jarrow sat on a stool close to his friend before replying.
'God, man! Thought the heat must 'have died down by now.' He laughed loudly. 'It must be nigh on three years ago.' Bert nodded in agreement and the two men talked for an hour of old times. Occasionally they laughed aloud at a remembered event or jest.

When Geordie had first arrived to work on the dockside Bert had taken a liking to him. He had been eager to learn and with his long lanky legs and a promising fighter build, the young lad from the Tyne would go far in the docklands.

Full of ale and in good humour the friends left the Dog and Gun as the landlord was closing the serving hatch. They walked, talked, and continued to laugh and shout in merriment to Bert's front door. Dogs barked as they passed by, and women shouted for them to be quiet, but the two companions were in such a good mood that nothing bothered them. As they neared Bert's home Big Geordie was about to turn and leave Bert to find lodgings for the night, but Bert insisted that he was to stay with him.

❋ ❋ ❋

'It may be a bit of a hovel.' He declared. 'But there's always a place for you Man.' He pulled his friend noisily through the doorway. As they entered there was movement in the darkened room and a child began to cry. A hushing and humming voice quietened the child and if the two men had been less rowdy, they would have heard the child suckling. The men staggered through the darkened room and moved on into the bedroom reserved for Bert and his two eldest lads. The youngsters were asleep in the corner of the room on a narrow box bed, sleeping 'top 'n' tail'. The large iron bed was empty, Nell had not occupied the marital bed for years, she curled up with Cissy and Alice in the other room.

Once in the relative privacy of the bedroom, Bert lit a candle and Geordie sat on the chair that usually held Bert's hastily removed clothes.

'Can we talk, private like?' Geordie pointed to the two sleeping boys.

'Yeah. Those two are dead to the world. Why?' Bert looked puzzled.

'I've got a job for yer' Geordie leaned forward taking up a pose of conspiracy. 'On me travels, I learnt a few things like up at the Manor House down Ayton way there is going to be a wedding.'

'Yeah! So what? I 'ope yer don't think I'm up to skivvying at a wedding' Bert interrupted. Geordie lifted his hands to calm his friend's irritation.

'Where there is a wedding there's gifts. Yeah!' Bert nodded. 'Well, I got on with this lass who is a housemaid there. All right was Moll, a grand lass.' His mind wandered as he remembered Moll's ample figure, bonny face, and willingness. 'Anyway,' He continued. 'she said that this rich Aunt of the bride was sending some family silver over as a wedding present. 'Course Moll went into detail, but the fact is that this silver will have to come through the docks, there'll be about five crates of the stuff.' Bert was still looking blankly at Geordie. He shook his big head disbelieving his friend's confusion. 'Yer sees, I know when, where and how this precious cargo is coming. I was telling the lads down the Crown about it, and they think it could be a good haul.' Still, Bert didn't understand what Geordie was trying to infer. Geordie stood up and crossed to sit by his friend. 'So, Bonny lad, are you going to help shift this cargo to a place where it will be more appreciated?' He pushed his face into Bert's and put his huge muscular arms around Bert's shoulders, jerking the smaller man's frame.

'Oh!' Suddenly Bert understood as the message reach his ale-fuddled brain.

'Good God man, the ale has got to yer head.'

'Yeah! I mean no! I just didn't see what you were getting at.'

'Right. Are you with us then?' Geordie emphasised the outright question.

'Course I am.' With lowered voices, they made their plans.

❊ ❊ ❊

The night was dark; clouds covered the sky hiding the moonlight. Big Geordie stood against the wharf, leaning nonchalantly, feet crossed and smoking a well-rolled cigarette. He watched the shadowy figure of Bert walk towards him and the two men greeted one another with a nod.

'All set for the night?'

'Aye!' Bert replied. 'The young 'ns will keep watch.'

Pacing up and down young Albert kept himself warm against the cold February air. He had a keen eye and enthusiasm for the task. It seemed hours since his father had left him at the dock gates, yet it was only 30 minutes. 'Give a good whistle son if you see the guard.' His father had instructed him. Albert had agreed without delay, he was proud that his father had chosen him for this task. He felt grown up and one of the 'men' at last. His dad had promised him a shilling if he did well, easy money after working six in the morning until eight at night over in the pottery. He still had the painful reminders of the hot ovens on his wrists and upper arms. Having to drag the saggars out whilst the ovens were still hot, the other lads had been prepared with old cloths wrapped around their arms to offer protection, but he had been young and gullible when he first started and knew nothing of the terrors of the kilns.

He had been pacing up and down for about an hour when he heard the guard approach. He began to peer under and around the huge packing cases as if searching for something.

'What are you doing in here young fella?' The guard was old, about fifty Albert guessed. Not much of a threat to an intruder, but he did have a large baton.

'I'm looking for me dog, mister.' Albert looked straight at the guard completely unafraid and confident. Saw 'im come in 'ere.' He put his forefinger and little finger against his tongue and blew a sharp piercing whistle. 'Here boy!' He bellowed and then whistled again. He shook his head and began to look around the packing cases once more for his imaginary dog. The guard placed his hand on the boy's shoulder.

'Are you sure he came in here?'

'Aye, 'e's a little shaggy pup, a sort of brown with black patches. My dad threw a boot at 'im for messing on the floor 'and he runs off.' Albert was beginning to enjoy the charade. The guard smiled and then began to help look for the puppy. After a few moments, Albert shook his head and said. 'I think I'll go 'an see if 'e 'as run back 'ome. Me dad will 'ave a go at me if I stay out any longer.'

'If I see the pup, shall I keep him here for you?' The guard asked the retreating boy.

'Aye' Albert shouted over his shoulder. 'Tie 'im up for me an' I'll check back the morra.' Albert grinned as he ran off towards home leaving the guard to look for a small shaggy pup that had never been near the docks.

Meanwhile deep among the packing cases and bales Big Geordie and the boy's father were loading wooden packing cases onto a flat cart. The horse's hooves were covered with rags to muffle the sound of its shoes on the cobbles. They had worked quickly and quietly. Only taking selected cases, which Geordie had marked with a chalk cross earlier that day while unloading from the ship. He had gotten Moll to innocently show him how the name of the house looked when written, believing that he was keen to learn to read and write.

As they lifted the fourth case, they heard the whistle. Geordie nodded to his partner in crime and climbed aboard the cart. Bert picked up a smaller case and was about to load it onto the cart when the second whistle sounded. The cart moved forward as he lowered the case, it missed its target and teetered on the edge of the cart for a second before crashing to the floor, breaking open and spilling the contents about Bert's feet. Geordie continued his way, oblivious to the scene he left behind in his haste.

Bert stood motionless staring down at the spilt silver. Knives, forks, and other tableware lay around him covered here and there in protective straw from the case. Fortunately for

Bert, the straw had dulled the crashing sound and as the preoccupied guard was talking to the boy the noise had gone unnoticed. For a moment Bert considered picking up the spilt silver.

Torn with indecision he eventually crouched down and stuffed the pockets of his overcoat with as much as he could, then he placed some smaller items into his trouser pockets. The calling and whistling for Albert's imaginary dog came closer and Bert stood and turned to make his getaway. As he went to make his escape his foot slipped on a cylindrical silver napkin ring, pulling at his ankle and knee. He saved himself from falling face down on the wet cobbles by thrusting out his hands. As his hands hit the cold floor, he felt a sharp pain in his groin and a warm stickiness trickled down his inner thigh. Shaking his head and swearing an oath at his clumsiness he got to his feet and staggered into the shadows.

Bert found his son in the pre-arranged meeting place, behind the church wall surrounding the small graveyard, which once served the small riverside parish, now surrounded by this ever-growing industrial town. Albert sat crouched down with his back against the wall looking down the street towards the dock road. His father staggered drunkenly towards him, and Albert simply stood up, his mouth agape at the sight of his father. With Bert dragging his injured foot and using the graveyard wall to aid his progress father and son made slow progress towards home.

The boy walked holding his father around the waist and the man leaning heavily on his son's shoulder, head hung low. It was obvious to those who passed the couple that young Albert was again helping his drunken father home.

Pained and angry Bert reached home, Albert pushed open the door and almost carried his father to the table. Bert collapsed onto the chair and bellowed out to Alice for help, she rose from the bed where minutes earlier she had slept with her sister and mother. Thinking her father was drunk she raked at the dying embers of the fire and placed the kettle into the hottest part. He rarely drank the tea she prepared on these occasions, but he always demanded the brew.

'Alice, Dad's hurt.' Albert's voice pleaded with concern for his dad. He may have been fearful of his dad, but he also loved him. Bert lay with his head on the table groaning. There was a dark patch seeping into the cloth of his trousers. He placed his hands into his coat pocket and began to empty the contents onto the table. After this, he put his hands into his trouser pocket and pulled out more sliver teaspoons. The first item he took out caused him to cry out in agony. Two small prongs of a small pastry fork had pierced the flesh in his groin and the larger sharp knifed prong had cut deeper into his flesh as he had walked
home.

He forced his fist into the wound to stem the flow of blood that oozed faster once the fork had gone. Swiftly Alice poured the hot water from the kettle into a bowl and went to tend to her father. Bert roughly pushed her away from him when she knelt beside him to clean his wound. Albert took the cloth from his sister and continued to tend to his dad, who did not object to his son's touch.

With a great amount of effort, Albert managed to get Bert undressed and onto his bed. He stemmed the bleeding using a towel bound with strips of sheeting. He poured a large tumbler of whisky; his father drank it down in one before collapsing back onto the pillows and falling into an exhausted sleep.

For five days Bert lay on his bed. His ankle had swollen to twice its natural size and his thigh and groin were bruised and swollen. Albert had stayed with him, seeing to his every need. He fetched and carried for him, feeding him broth and whiskey, emptying the chamber pot and running errands. Big Geordie had visited the day after, but Bert had still been in a drunken sleep.

On his second visit, Alice opened the door in answer to the loud banging to find the huge man looking at her. His crooked leer caused her to shudder; there was something in his demeanour that Alice found distasteful and frightening. Her father's drinking companions would always remain strangers to her, those she had met all stank of stale beer and smoke, had two or three days of beard growth and wore greasy caps over their unkempt hair.

She was meeting a man who would play a big part in her life but she would not realise for years how big a part that would be. He, on the other hand, noticed her and liked what he saw. She was so petite next to his height and breadth, that he wanted to crouch down and sweep her up she was so pretty. Her huge brown eyes looked up at him soulfully out of her pale creamy skin. Once she had rounded out a bit, he would see a fine lass. Without greeting the visitor, she stood to one side while he passed her and went into the bedroom.

His huge frame filled the doorway of the small bedroom, looking down on the invalid he greeted his friend.

'God, man! What the bleedin' 'ell 'append?' He dropped heavily onto the side of the bed causing Bert to wince. 'By man, that's a grand lass you 'ave there. Nice to look at ain't she?' He winked and punched Bert in the ribs in a friendly gesture, Bert winced again and pulled his face in response to the pain. 'Sorry, Bert. Bet you are 'urtin a bit, eh?' He pulled a bottle out of his overcoat pocket. 'Brought you summit to ease the pain and to toast our good fortune.'

Smiling slyly Bert accepted the gift, he had no intention to share the extra silver he had taken; he had suffered for those last bits of cutlery. No, he would keep his own little nest egg as insurance. As they celebrated, he was blissfully unaware of four small spoons missing from Bert's treasure.

FOUR

The pain in Bert's groin had eased enough for him to bear sitting at the table. As he sipped his tea, he looked across at his wife. Now he had the time to study her he could see there was still no improvement in her mental state. She had taken to wandering around the streets, why or where was anyone's guess because the stupid woman certainly could not tell you. One of the children went out to find her if she did not return within an hour of her leaving her chair in the corner. Bert could not understand her at all.

Alice was preparing a meal, busily in and out of the scullery. Bert was becoming increasingly frustrated at his inability to get out of this poky room. The lad had kept him going with jugs of ale and news from the dock lads, he hated having to rely on Albert. He could never work again on the dockside, certainly not doing the heavy lifting and labouring which was all he knew. He did not have a trade and he could neither read nor write. He would have to rely on others to put food in his mouth and ale in his glass and that meant putting all the brats to work.

Of course, he would get an odd job but that would have to be light. Cursing his stupidity, he was looking for someone to blame for his misfortunes.

The baby Flo began to whimper for attention. Now nine months old she had to be bound to the chair leg with a sheet to stop her from crawling around. The infant was feeling as cross and frustrated as Bert. She struggled to free herself, crying louder and louder in a temper that aroused Bert's annoyance. He screamed at her.

'Shut up for God's sake.' However, this did not affect the child, she just cried louder. Alice entered from the scullery and tried to pacify the child, but Flo had reached screaming and would not quieten. Bert snarled at Alice, cursing her as a useless good for nothing. He picked up the heavy breadboard that had laid on the table for the meal and threw it at the child, he did not aim however, it hit the baby on the head with a heavy sickening thud. Flo collapsed into her mother's arms unconscious. The sudden silence overpowered the room.

Alice with a mother's instinct retrieved the board and flung it back towards Bert. Her aim was poor, and it whistled past his head and bounced off the wall behind him onto the floor.

'Bastard.' She cried out. 'There was no need for that.' She rarely raised her voice and had never used bad language before, even though she had heard vulgar words from the surrounding adults. Her father's behaviour had incensed her to such a degree that she no longer feared the outcome of her outburst. Quickly she had untied the child and tried to rouse her. Flo's body began to shudder and jerk, her eyes opened wide, and she made dreadful gurgling sounds in her throat as she went into a fit. Terrified by this Alice grabbed the child into her arms and ran from the house.

Bert, stared at the door after Alice's rapid exit, stunned into silence, he had woken a spirit in Alice he never thought she had. Left alone with his wife and his meal still not ready, he limped back into his bedroom and lay on the bed. He felt no remorse for his behaviour, the child should learn to be quiet and not make such a row. He considered for a moment the child's shaking jerky movements. One of the young lads down at the docks threw one of those fits once. He's in the poor house now or was he dead, Bert was unsure. His thoughts led him back to the child. Had he killed her? He didn't think so. Youngsters bounce back. He had bounced back after blows from his dad; it was Alice's response that had disturbed him the most. Fancy, her shouting out like that; he would never think she had the courage. What if the child died? His thoughts returned to the real issue. What if he were responsible? No. He would deny everything. The child fell against the fender. Inwardly cursing Flo for making him angry he reached for a bottle of whisky that he kept under his bed and took a good swallow of the calming amber liquid. Suitably relaxed and his conscience cleared he lay down and waited for his supper to be ready.

Tess Harvey had calmly sponged the baby's face and body with cold water whilst Alice cried over the child.

"E shouldn't 'ave done that. If 'E's killed her?' She pleaded with Tess Harvey for assurance that it would be all right. 'Don't fret Alice. She's all right, just shocked. Look she's waking up.' The older woman tried to hide her concern from this young mother. She has gone through enough tragedy without this, she thought. Oh! How she hoped this baby would be OK if she were to take regular fits, they may affect her for life. The baby's fit eased and Flo when into a peaceful natural sleep.

'She should sleep now, Alice. I'll lay her down on my bed and keep an eye on her. You go and rescue that meal.' She took the sleeping child and lay her down on the soft mattress. As she stroked the child's head, she could feel the dent in the back of the skull that the breadboard had left on its impact, biting her lip she said a silent prayer. Alice tearfully returned to peeling the vegetables.

* * *

She poured the watery soup into bowls for the children and her mother. The few vegetables and rabbit meat which lay in the bottom of the pan would be reheated for the two older boys and their father. Albert and Joe walked in together; both looked worn out and covered in the clay dust that gathered on every part of them whilst at work in the local pottery. They sat on the bench and ate hungrily at the stew and bread. Albert took two coins from his pocket and handed them to Alice, taking the cue from his brother, Joe also gave her his wages. She slipped the coins into her apron pocket just as her father exited from his bedroom. Alice glanced in his direction with lowered lids and tight lips. She hoped he had not noticed her putting the coins away if he had ever found her hiding place for the housekeeping money she knew where it would end up. Bert sat at the table and enjoyed his meal.

Big Geordie had become a frequent visitor to Victoria Street and always during the meagre evening meal, which Alice then had to draw out even further. Money had always been tight but now Bert was unable to work due to his injury, and fewer coins came her way. The boy's wages went a little way to paying the rent, but Albert kept quite a bit of his wage back for his own pleasure; Alice knew that he gave a little to his father for a drink.

One evening, as usual, the big docker sat at the table enjoying mutton stew and fresh bread. Bert sat at the head of the table watching the family. Alice was looking thin and pale; he hadn't bothered with her of late as his 'urges' had declined since his 'accident'. She was colder towards him since the incident with Flo. The fits occurred on a regular basis now and it was quite frightening to watch. Alice was not caring for the child correctly, or it had caught something from its poor mad grandmother.

His two eldest had already bolted down the meat and were now supping noisily at their weak tea. Next to Alice, in contrast to her sister Cissy was becoming bonnier each day. She still did not have womanly curves, but she promised to be a real beauty, he pursed his lips in appreciation of her looks then glanced at the two youngest boys. They sat close together opposite Geordie, slowly eating the stew, trying to make the meat last and relishing every mouthful. Both boys were still small for their ages, thin and pale-faced like their elder sister. Bert would never understand these two lads. He could not look at them without feeling slightly fearful of them. They were too close, almost bound together like a freak he had seen at a fair, two heads and bodies joined at the hip. What they had was unnatural somehow, but he could not figure out what. These two younger lads were always whispering together, collaborating, and sneaking about all the time. They never looked him in the eye and were always running off somewhere secretively. They were so unlike the two older boys, now they would grow to be fine men, especially Albert. One day he would get their measure, but right now he had other plans for them

They ate the meal in silence, this now broken when Bert asked Geordie,

'Did you find anything Geordie?'

'Oh! Aye! I nearly forgot.' He looked around the table to make sure they were all listening to him. 'Sonny Porter is looking for a couple of lads. I told him about these two.' He pointed to the two youngest boys waving a slice of bread around in the process. The lads stared at the big fellow, wide-eyed and fearful of the fate there knew was about to befall them. 'They're just about the right size, 'n the money would come in useful, eh?' He nodded to Bert.

'Aye,' Bert agreed eagerly. His face dulled for a moment before adding. 'Thought 'e 'ad some lads?'

'Yeh but one of 'em as outgrown the chimneys, and 'e lost two with pneumonia or summat.' Replied Geordie.

Alice was on her feet, leaning with both her hands palm down on the table she pleaded.

'You can't do that! They'd never cope.'

'Mind yer own business our Alice. They'd be good chimney lads. Neither of 'em is strong enough for ᶦbarra boys' down at the steelworks and that's the only other option open around 'ere.' Bert's glower did not deter her. 'It's either that or the saggar ovens. At least at Parker's, it's a live-in job so we won't have to feed them.'

'But Sonny Parker goes through his lads. They never last more than six months' She leaned even closer to this man she hated but had to call father. Bert stood up and matched her pose.

'Shut up girl.' He said with a low quiet yet commanding tone. 'They'll do as I say and that's an end to it.' The tension and raised voices had aroused Nell, who until this time had sat quietly drinking soup from a chipped cup and dreaming of faraway places. She began to moan and rock. Alice motioned to Cissy to deal with her and pacify their mother. The two boys had sat quietly throughout the noisy exchange, keeping their thoughts to themselves, they were dealing with this news the best way they could. They would support one another through any crisis; for as long as they were together, they could see anything through.

Alice though, was determined that this would be one thing her father was not going to get away with.

'We can manage with what we have. I'll take in washing if I must.' She was feeling very brave and added. 'You only want the money for beer. Can't you use your little treasure trove for that?' Alice dodged the bowl which flew across the room and crashed against the wall, splattering the remains of Bert's dinner over Nell and Flo. Bert shook his fist at Alice then turned to Geordie.

'Do it Geordie. Tell Sonny can 'ave 'em.' Geordie was frowning at Bert. This was a different side to his friend, a violent side. Most men of his class had a temper, but the lass was only trying to help. 'What had the lass meant about treasure troves?' he thought to himself.

Alice sat down in defeat.

❊ ❊ ❊

Later that evening Bert and Geordie were sitting in the Dog and Gun enjoying a pint of beer.

'What was your Alice on about?' Geordie asked Bert.

'She's going daft like her mother, take no notice.' Bert looked down into his glass trying to be nonchalant. The last thing he wanted was for this big fellow to find out he'd kept something back. He would be sure to demand a share; however, Geordie was o fool.

'Come off it, your Alice is far from daft. She's got a stronger head on her shoulders than you give her credit for.' He glowered at Bert, now he knew he was hiding something. 'Have you told her about the job we did?' Bert thought quickly.

'Well, she guessed I'd been up to something, as you said she isn't too daft' He laughed nervously. 'Mind I haven't told her it was silver, and I haven't been exactly out on a spending spree?' Bert looked up into Geordie's face and stared at him, daring him to doubt his word. Geordie stepped back slightly from the foul breath; Bert's face was that close it may have looked as if the smaller man was intimidating him to an onlooker, however Big Geordie was not that easily frightened. Geordie raised his hands in mock terror.

'Take it easy old man! It's not that easy to shift quality stuff like that.' Geordie's grin was a sneer. 'Freddie is still trying to get the best deal.' He was beginning to see this man in his true light, and he didn't like it at all. As a workmate he was fine, but after seeing how he treated his family, especially Alice, he held him in complete contempt. Geordie may be a big man in stature, but his heart was soft, and looking at Alice softened it further.

'Well, if I don't get cash soon for that job, we'll all be out on our ears. The rents well overdue, I will 'ave to put some money over soon.' His lies flowed so easily. Bert swallowed his beer and motioned to the bartender at the serving hatch for more. 'If I can throw some cash on the table Alice will keep quiet.' He wiped his mouth with his sleeve. Geordie knew Bert was talking nonsense, Alice would be lucky to get a copper a week off her father, even with the windfall, he was due.

'Will yer still send the boys to Sonny?' He was wishing he had never said he would help place the youngsters.

'Oh! Aye! Them nosey lot down our street know I can't work. I'll 'ave to let 'em think I'm getting money from somewhere.' Bert nudged Geordie in the ribs playfully. 'Meanwhile throw some money over that hatch.' He was confident that he had thrown his friend off the scent regarding his 'insurance^s. Geordie was still suspicious; he knew how Bert had hurt himself making his escape. Apparently slipping and falling against a hook, true the cobbles were always slippery and greasy, but he was sure no hook had caused Bert's injury. He knew he would never get to the bottom of this 'accident', so he chose to remain quiet for the time being.

FIVE

L ife at Victoria Street went on through the summer without a word from Eddie and George. Flo, now nearing her second birthday was toddling around clumsily. She still had fits, but these were now fewer and usually happened when overexcited or upset. Alice had learnt to cope very well with the occasional fit.

It was washing day and Alice was busy with Cissy in the small yard, Cissy stood on an upturned bucket so that she could reach the poss-tub. Alice heaved at the rusty handle forcing the wet sheets through the well-worn mangle. The old rollers had worn down in the centre from use, but if she folded the sheets into a thick wad then water would press out of the fabric. The old woollen scarf wrapped around the broken handle went a little way to prevent the hard metal from biting into her hands. Flo played noisily with a tin pan and a dozen stones. In and out of the pan the stones clattered. Cissy was becoming agitated with the racket.

'Oh, Our Alice, can't she do that a bit quieter? It echoes right round this yard.'

'Leave her be while she's happy,' Alice replied without even looking up at her sister.

'Should I go and look for Mam, she's been gone ages?'

'No. We must get these done and hung out if we want to get them back on the beds.' Cissy sighed heavily, she hated wash day with Alice, there was no gossip or laughter like at the communal washtubs.

✽ ✽ ✽

Nell had left the house to use the earth toilet called the 'netty' earlier that morning and had not yet returned. She did not lose her way as much as lose interest, she left the small yard behind her and began to walk without direction, wearing the cape her mother had made for her sixteenth birthday. It was beautifully stitched and quilted in the Italian style. The rose-pink, silk sateen fabric, was delicately embroidered with pure white roses and swirled stalks. The lining was made from one of her mother's voluptuous petticoats, soft Egyptian cotton.

The cape felt soft and warm against her neck. Now faded and worn with the stitching broken away in places it hung lopsided. Alice had tried to wash it and it shrank against the quitting, looking puckered and miss shaped. Neil went everywhere with this piece of 'rag', as her husband had called it. To Nell's eyes, it was still as new. As she walked the streets, in her poor demented state it was still her sixteenth birthday and she was walking on the hills with her father, whilst her mother prepared a special birthday tea. She had promised that she would never be without this beautiful gift, and she would keep it forever. This promise, she had kept. It had broken her mother's heart when Nell had worn the cape over her shoulders on her wedding day, that fateful day when the sham marriage took place. Nell's swelling stomach showing under the folds of her mother's wedding dress. Watching her lovely daughter taken by that rough, uncouth individual left an emptiness in her heart. She despised herself and her husband for allowing it to happen. They should have curbed her walking out with this man and not given in to her pleading like a child. She was their only living child, the light of their life.

The newlyweds headed into the bustling town away from

the peace of the Yorkshire dales and Nell's loving parents. They would never see her smiling face again.

Nell's mind had shut out her marriage and the dreadful life, which had followed. The dark miserable days which had followed the birth of her daughter. The depression had encroached hon er after each birth until she had happily slipped into denial. She now lived in hen world where no harm could come to her.

As she walked, she felt the soft green grass at her feet, not hard uneven cobbles. The heavy smoke-filled air from the surrounding industry smelt of freshly mown grass and rose petals to her senses. If she looked up, she could see a warm early autumn sun, light fluffy clouds rushing by on the wind, birds singing and children laughing in the distance. She walked and skipped like a young girl, swirling around on tiptoe and swinging her arms about. Smiling with contentment she looked behind her in response to a voice calling for her to wait. Mischievously she ran a little way from the voice, and then stopped in order that her companion could catch her. As she stood waiting her eye caught a bright golden object reflecting in the watery sunlight. She bent to pick it up. Holding it high she exclaimed

'Oh! Father isn't it beautiful?'

A voice replied impatiently. 'Yes Nell, pure treasure.' Nell nodded in agreement and clasped the gold buckle to her. 'Come along dear!' A hand grasped Nell's cape took her arm and turned her towards home.' Everyone will be worried if we don't reach home soon.' Nell put her arm through her father's, and they walked home. She chatted all the way about insignificant childish things. How her friend Betty had a new dress, and it did not suit her at all. Polly's brother had gone to school in York, and it would be nice if she could have tea with the Chapmans again, such a lovely family.

On reaching home she skipped gaily into the yard, over the step and into the house. Alice looked up from the mangle when she heard her mother's voice and opened the yard gate.

Walking arm and arm towards her were Nell and Tess Harvey. As soon as her mother was safe in the yard Alice spoke.

'Where did you find her?' She asked.

'Top end of Coronation Road heading for the dock gates.' Replied Tess. Alice remarked that her mother had to be holding something.' She's picked up a rusty old buckle as treasure. She'll discard it soon as children do.' Tess Harvey recognised that Nell was in her second childhood and quite harmless. She did not understand mental illness and its complications, but she knew Nell was a soul in need of care and Alice in need of a friend. It was a full-time job caring for this poor demented woman and Alice also had to cook and clean for the rest of the family. Added to this the burden of a young baby made a heavy yoke for Alice to bear.

Nell returned to her seat by the fire, the cape lay across her lap. She fingered the fine embroidery as she rocked in the chair, staring into the embers of the fire. In the bright red glow, she saw pictures of the past, memories that she lost herself in.

* * *

the yard, Tess stood arms folded across her ample bosom and leant against the wall. She watched Cissy at the line pegging out the shabby sheets across the narrow alleyway. Alice was wringing out a few final items from the wash basket. Flo had ceased the noisy game; instead, she had found a puddle of water fascinating, slapping the water with a flat hand, giggling as the dirty water splashed into her face.

'Cissy's growing fast Alice.' Tess Harvey said without looking away from the girl hanging the washing out. 'She's a good help to you, isn't she?' Alice shrugged her shoulders but did not answer the neighbour's question. Tess turned to look at Alice. 'You know I've been teaching her to sew?' Alice nodded. 'Not that she needs much teaching she's very good, very neat and thorough.' Alice looked up at the woman before picking up the basket of wet clothes then went ahead to take the basket to Cissy. As she passed Tess Harvey she said.

'To be perfectly honest, I couldn't do without her.' She walked over to Cissy and swapped the empty basket by her sister's feet for the full one. When she entered the yard again Tess had crouched down by the now very wet child. The sight amused Alice. 'Looks like Flo has learnt to wash herself; I wish she were as keen to let me wash her face.' Tess picked up the wet toddler and handed her to Alice.

'I'll come straight to the point Alice.' Tess took a deep breath. 'I would like Cissy to come to me so that she can start an apprenticeship with Miss Wrightson, the seamstress on Diamond RD.' Tess lifted her hands in a gesture to prevent Alice from interrupting. 'Please hear me out, Miss Wrightson is expanding and opening a Salon. She is looking for an apprentice and I was telling her about Cissy. It'll mean long hours, but she would learn a trade.' Alice stood quiet looking at this kind neighbour who had loved and cared for Cissy since she had learnt to toddle.

Tess had taken to Cissy from the first time she had seen her on Alice's hip. Alice would have been seven when Cissy was born and as she had with all her brothers and sis ters, she at once became her surrogate mother, seeing to her every need. Cissy was a beautiful baby with nature to match. She had rarely cried and always had a smile for the faces that would look her way. As soon as she could walk Tess had taken her out on trips and gave her treats to share with her siblings. Cissy was the replacement for the daughter Tess Harvey had lost to cholera at two years old. She never had any more children and Alice did not know what had happened to Mr Harvey.

Tess was almost pleading for Alice to allow Cissy to take up the apprenticeship and live with her. Alice was now shaking her head.

'I'm sorry but you can see how I'm fixed.' Alice had Flo on her hip and the empty basket in hand as she walked into the scullery with Tess Harvey walking behind her.

'OK. So, you will not let her come to me, but will you think about the apprenticeship? It would be so good for her.' Tess continued. Alice stood in the doorway leading to the main house, she bit at her lip deep in thought. 'The money would certainly be useful.'

Tess looked expectantly at the young woman who had her precious Cissy's future in her hands. 'No. I can't let her go.' Tess sighed heavily at the rejection.

'Well, OK if she can't come to me will you still think about the job?' She placed her hand lightly on Alice's arm to prevent her from walking away. Alice turned to look at this kind woman. She knew that Tess was keen to see Cissy out of this poverty and make something of her. When Alice nodded in agreement Tess grinned like the cat with the cream. Just then Cissy entered the scullery and the two adults stopped talking and Alice mashed some well-earned tea for them all.

That evening after the meal was over and the dishes cleared away, Alice sat at the table and told Cissy of the plans Tess Harvey had for her. She omitted the part about Cissy lodging with Tess, as she knew Cissy would be disappointed at her refusal to allow it.

'What will Dad say?' Cissy asked.

'What he doesn't know won't 'urt.' Bert, as usual, had gone to the alehouse with Geordie and had taken the eldest lad Albert with him as a treat. Alice continued in a lowered voice. If we keep this to ourselves, we will be able to keep your wage quiet. We need the money more than he does.' Cissy was nodding in agreement. 'You'll be out of here before he even gets up and you'll be back before he comes in, so he won't miss you.'

'Our Albert might.' Cissy frowned at her sister. 'He'll tell dad.'

'You leave Albert to me; I'll tell him some story to cover it up,' Cissy said excitedly.

'When do I start?' She was keen to begin.

'Next week. Tess Harvey will take you to the rear of the Salon and show you the ropes.' Alice looked over her sister's attire. 'We'll have to find a dress that fits. The one you have is showing a bit too much leg.' Cissy grinned mischievously.

'Mrs Harvey and me 'ave been busy. She got a nice dress from the flea market an' she's been showing how to sew by altering it to fit me. It looks nice now.' Cissy was quite pleased with herself. Alice smiled at her sister's eagerness and enthusiasm, would she be as chirpy after a few early mornings and late nights?

Alice need not have worried about Cissy. The other workers in the establishment soon saw Cissy's charm, and they were all truly kind to her. They were also fearful of upsetting Tess Harvey; she was a very imposing figure in the workroom. Tess had worked for Miss Wrightson on a casual basis for years and many of the women in the salon had Tess to thank for their jobs. It was prudent to stay in favour of this formidable woman. Miss Wrightson soon saw Cissy's potential and congratulated Tess on finding such a talented youngster.

As Alice had guessed her father did not notice any difference in the running of the household. However, Albert had seen a change in his younger sister and was curious when finding her dressed in the mornings. He was sure she had a new dress, and it was not one of Alice's cast-offs, he had not seen this one before. He asked Alice why Cissy was up so early on a morning, and she told him that Cissy was ten now and expected to help more around the house, and she was to run errands.

Another time she said that Cissy was going to the school just opened. He did not believe that story at all. He had mentioned that the school cost money, but Alice had said Cissy was doing errands for the Misses in return for lessons. This he accepted as more credible and did not ask anymore, but he remained suspicious, why was she dressed in good clothes instead of the usual shabby print dress and pinafore? Something funny was going on and he would find out eventually.

Joe Allerton did not bother with such trivialities of the household. He was past his fifteenth birthday and was too busy worrying about how his own life was going. He was still pushing trucks in the pottery while his brother; only a year older than him was learning a potter's trade. Albert had proved to be a lazy worker, but he had the guile and cunning to hide this from his employers. All the potters liked Albert; he was quite a character around the pottery, always making the men laugh with his antics, often quite dangerous. The youngsters would get injured when Albert jumped out at a truck pusher and caused the clay pots to tumble to the floor. Naturally, he had left the scene before trouble ensued upon the poor youngster for breaking valuable merchandise.

Albert had now risen in the ranks to a potter's apprentice, which meant more money. He had not informed his father of this and had threatened Joe with a good pasting if he told anyone. He made the best of his position and soon became very friendly with the others he worked with. At sixteen he was thin and wiry like his father, but it appeared that he would be taller than his dad by the time he had finished growing. Already he was five-foot-tall, and his trousers stood two inches from the top of his clogs. He took after his father in looks and people would say that he was his father's double. A sharp angular face with piercing blue eyes topped with straight hair that was almost black. He was quick on his feet, sly and cunning. The most important people in his life were his father and himself, and he was particularly good at looking after both.

Joe was quite different in both stature and temperament, stocky and not very tall. Although he was born a year after his brother, he was more mature and thoughtful. His features were softer than Albert's and would make him a very handsome young man. He had large blue eyes and a shock of thick wavy blond hair. Alice cut his hair for him regularly, but it grew so fast that it always looked untidy. When his work was over for the day, he could be found breathing the fresh air that could only be found at the top of the highest hill, well above the smog and smoke that hung over the industrial town below. He would walk the hills, walking further and higher each day. His young body was growing strong muscles and bones. His senses appreciated the birdsong and smells which were so different from the stench of the gutters in the town. He loved to be alone on the hills, the peace and quietness soothed him, and he felt free.

Today he had decided he would forgo his walk on the hills and instead enquire at the steelworks for a better job. He felt the need to get away from the pottery and the influence of his brother. If he could get away from that environment, he knew he would be able to enjoy his life. Once away from Albert and his bullying, he would have all he needed. A job, a roof over his head, such as it was, and the hills to walk. So, he headed away from the pottery and towards his future. He had heard from George Firman, one of the shift leaders in the furnace room, that there was work there for a fit, young lad.

He made his way down Pearl Street and onto the main road through the town, passing the shops and offices that were now closing their doors at the end of a long day. As he came to the end of the long road leading away from the town square, he noticed Cissy. She was exiting from one of the many alleyways that lead to the rear of the shops. Walking alongside her were a few other young lasses, Mrs Harvey and another middle-aged woman. He had an idea that Cissy was earning but had not pressed the matter, as he did not consider it any of his business.

Joe caught up to the group of women and tapped Cissy on the shoulder. She jumped like a startled rabbit and turned to see Joe's laughing face.

'Oh, our Joe, don't do that.' She thumped him playfully on the arm as she spoke. She liked Joe, probably because he was nearer to her age and nothing like Albert whom she never trusted.

'Sorry, Ciss.' He looked at her companions, ignoring the fact that Cissy had been leaving work; he still thought it was none of his business. Mrs Harvey, he knew of course, but the girl stood next to her he had never met. He looked at the pretty face as he said to Cissy. 'Are you gonna introduce your friends Cissy?' She proudly announced the workmates one by one. 'This is Betty, Mrs Harvey you know.' She turned to the girls in the group. 'Agnes, Ada and Martha.' Joe nodded to each of them, but his eyes went back to the lovely face of Agnes.

'Now then Joe" Tess Harvey's greeting to Joe was more like a warning to leave them alone.

'Don't worry, I won't tell.' He assured Tess with a wink, and she believed him. Tess turned back towards Cissy.

'Come along, we must be getting home.' Cissy trotted off behind Tess and the rest of the group followed. Agnes hung back for just a second or two when her eyes met those of Joe's she blushed prettily, smiled at him then followed her companions. Joe was very flattered and smiled back rakishly.
'Wow,' He thought 'l must get to know her.'

Once the group had left his sight, he continued his way to the steelworks. He still had quite a way to go, and he must get there before the shift finished if he were to see George Firman, so he quickened his pace, spurred on by the thought of Agnes.

SIX

Cissy had been working at the Salon for ten months and was still enjoying both the work and the company of the other girls. Joe did get his job in the steelworks, and now he was an apprentice to Bill Johnson in the furnace room. Albert had quickly lost interest in Cissy and her secret, instead, he had pursued the affections of a girl he had met at the pottery. She was a few years older than he was and very willing to teach Albert those things he could not learn at home. Unfortunately, her influence was not a good one. He stayed away from home most evenings and threw fewer coins on the table on payday.

Bert had exchanged his haul of silver into a cache of sovereigns and put it with the money he had eventually received from Geordie, this was a tidy sum. He spent it very carefully and very slowly, not wanting people to think he had come into money. He had taken the odd job on the dockside sweeping up and other light work so that he could justify the money he did spend. The few coins he threw on the table for Alice amounted to a pittance and she would certainly never have managed if she had not been getting Cissy's wages.

Joe was particularly good and gave her a little extra, but Bill Johnson and his wife had offered him lodgings with them. He had told Alice that he would continue to send her a little money each week. She did not want him to leave, but as Joe had pointed out, sleeping in the same room as his father and Albert was not ideal now that he was working shifts. Mrs Johnson had offered him a room of his own and meals. It would take the strain from Alice's shoulders, so she eventually agreed. He was to move out at the end of the week.

❋ ❋ ❋

The evening before Joe was to leave for his new lodgings, he was preparing to go for one of his walks. Alice was busy clearing away the supper dishes while Cissy refashioned one of her old dresses to fit Flo.

'While you're out Joe could you keep a lookout for Mam?' Alice asked.

'Of course, how long has she been out this time?'

'She left just before you came in from work, so maybe an hour,' Alice replied. 'She might be up at the cemetery. Mrs Nelson brought her back from there two nights in a row.'

'Well, the nights are light so I shouldn't have much trouble finding her. I'll try there first.' He left by the scullery door and was not aware of Bert, with Geordie in tow, entering by the other door in a foul temper.

Bellowing with rage and banging his fists on the table, his face red with anger, he shouted.

'I'll swing for 'em, I will.' Bert could not control his breathing; he was so angry. 'Make a bloody fool out of me will they.' Geordie was trying to calm him but was failing. Alice was terrified. She had not seen him as angry as this for a long time. Things had been going his way lately, he had gotten drunk often, but not in this state. He had not been out long enough to drink too much ale, so why the ranting and raving? While Bert continued to shout and bellow obscenities and making no sense Geordie spoke to Alice.

'The young 'uns 'ave gone.' He said to her. She stared at him incredulously, not understanding what he was saying. Bert turned on Alice.

'Yeh, You 'eard it. The little Sods 'ave bloody run away.' His voice got louder, and he banged his fist on the table and flung the stool across the room, which crashed into the fireplace. 'Sonny Parker wouldn't bloody pay me. Runaway 'e told me. They've bloody well run away. I'll skin them alive when I get hold of the brats.' He glowered into Alice's stricken face and spat pure venom at her. 'You knew, you did it,' She backed away from him as he bore down on her, pinning her to the wall. Alice was shaking her head in denial of the accusation mouthing 'No. No.' over again. As Bert neared her, he raised his fist and would have punched her in the face had Geordie not caught at his sleeve and pulled his arm down. He placed himself between Bert and his daughter.

'Give over, Man,' he pushed the smaller man in the chest causing him to stagger backwards. 'she knows nowt.'

'That bitch knows all right.' He tried to push past the big man. 'She took 'em, she never wanted 'em to go did she?' He pushed against Geordie again, determined to get at the terrified girl. With a hefty shove, Geordie pushed Bert back. 'Leave her alone!' Geordie's face was only inches away from Bert's as he snarled the words, pushing his hard, bony fingers into Bert's chest to emphasise each word. Alice's father deflated visibly in defeat against this huge frame blocking his advance. He raised his hand and lowered his head, but his face remained taught.

'Right, All right.' Bert backed away, and as he sat at the table, he growled. 'You would take her part, wouldn't yer?' He glowered at the man he had always thought of as his friend.

'Shut up Bert, blaming Alice won't find 'em.' Geordie stood guarding Alice against her father's wrath. 'Go 'n get yer coat 'n we'll go and look for 'em.' He spoke to Bert as a father would to an unruly child. Bert obliged grudgingly and snatched his overcoat from the hook on the back of the door, then slammed the door as he left the house. Geordie turned to Alice, He was still standing close enough to smell her odour, which he could never find offensive.

She stood still, her mouth slightly agape and her eyes wide with fear. He lifted his hand and gently stroked her cold cheek. 'Don't worry Lass.' He spoke softly, the words were meant to soothe her, but they had the opposite effect. She ducked away from him and darted to the other side of the room. With the table as a barrier between them, she felt a little safer. Shaking her head, she said with a quaking voice.

'Don't you touch me. Don't you ever touch me."

'I... I'm sorry Alice' he stammered. 'I never meant to frighten you.'

'Oh. Oh. I know what you meant to do."

'No. I told you. I won't let anyone hurt you.' Geordie said quietly, saddened that this lovely girl was frightened of him. He followed Bert out of the room.

Throughout this entire scene, Cissy sat scared and motionless. Flo had slept through it all; it took a lot to wake the child once asleep. Alice placed her hands flat on the table and slowly sat on the bench.
Shaking now with shock she looked across at her sister.

'Good God Cissy, what was that all about?' she asked. Cissy spurred on by her sister's need crossed to where she stood and placed her arms around her trembling shoulders to comfort her. 'They're out there somewhere Cissy. If Dad finds them, he will kill them, I know he will.'

'No, those two are clever. Dad won't find them.' Cissy assured her sister.

❊ ❊ ❊

Joe had found his mother in the cemetery as Alice had suggested. She was chatting to a stone angel who guarded a child in its final resting place. How serene and content his mother had looked as he approached her. He could not remember ever seeing her look so well. It was a warm summer evening, yet she still had the old cape over her shoulders. He could hear her speaking as if in prayer but as he became closer, he realised that she was talking to an imaginary companion. The words she said did not make sense to him. She was talking about 'golden wings' and 'treasures'. Laughing lightly and smiling up at the angel she stood and began to dance around childishly. Joe looked about in embarrassment, hoping that no one had seen her. However, they were quite alone, so gently he persuaded her to come home, and she obliged willingly at the promise of cool lemonade which would, of course, be nothing but water.

As he entered the house, he saw Cissy and Alice sipping tea. Both had been crying and Alice looked extremely upset. Nell went at once to the chair by the dying embers of the fire and smiled at the pictures she found there.

'What's wrong?' Joe asked the two girls. Cissy related the events of the past half-hour while he stood quiet and calmly. He did not utter a word but nodded his head when she had finished the tale then turned on his heels and left the house.

He knew the area and the hills better than most. He asked himself where the two boys would have run. Certainly, they would not stay around home and risk the wrath of their father. They would be hiding out somewhere. Had they planned their escape? Or just made a dash for freedom? If he knew the boys, he would have thought they had planned it.

He searched deserted shepherd's huts, haystacks and even the woods where the youngsters had spent time chasing rabbits. Joe searched all evening until the light began to fade, and then he checked the dockside before he returned home. There had been no ships in that day a friendly docker had told him. A couple of coal barges up and down the river and a ship was out in the bay waiting to come in. The man promised to keep an eye open for the two lads and Joe went home disappointed. By the time he reached home the house was in darkness. He stumbled through the scullery, falling over a wash basket. On entering the kitchen, he saw a shadowy figure slouched over the table. Quietly he sat by Alice and gently woke her.

'Come on lass, get yersel' to bed.' Alice looked up at her brother, her eyes were red from crying. Joe shook his head. 'Sorry I didn't find them.' He looked over his shoulder towards his father's bedroom. 'Did he find anything?"

'No, Geordie brought him home earlier with a load on. He didn't look for long. Had to carry him to bed.'

'Not much more to do tonight,' Joe told his sister to go to bed. 'I'm on an early shift tomorrow but I'll look again.' He gently pulled her to her feet and urged her again to go to bed.

* * *

The sun rose early but Joe had already left for work before Alice and Cissy had risen. They did not discuss the previous night's events as they prepared for the day's work. As Cissy was leaving the house, she looked at Alice, Flo had stirred and was winging for her breakfast.

'Shall I stay Alice?'

'You get yourself off to work, don't be worrying about me.' Alice knew why her sister was concerned.' He will sleep most of the day after the ale he drank. Do not dawdle or you'll be late. It's wash day so I'll need you to come straight home.' Cissy nodded then turned and left.

Tess Harvey was waiting for her on the doorstep and as Cissy approached her, her friend walked to meet her. It was their usual habit to have a drink of tea in Tess's kitchen before they headed off to work together, while Tess prepared some food for their breaks. This morning Tess hurried towards Cissy and on reaching her took her by the arm and led her hurriedly down the street. She greeted Cissy loudly.

'Morning Cissy. Come along now, we've no time to waste this morning.' Once around the corner and well out of earshot of any nosy neighbours Tess drew Cissy to an abrupt halt. She lowered her voice to a whisper. 'I had a couple of visitors last night.' Cissy's mouth dropped open and then snapped shut as she placed her hand over it to stop herself from crying out. Then she gave a heavy sigh of relief.

'They went to you then?'

'Aye, still covered in soot. Ground right in by the looks of it. I made them wash but I can tell you I wish I hadn't. They were covered in bruises, both of 'em. I swear the young 'un looks as if his arm is broken.' Tess took a breath and looked about to ensure no one was within earshot before continuing. 'Really painful it was when I was washing him. Kept holding his shoulder. He didn't cry though; they were both very brave.' She took hold of Cissy's arm again. 'We better keep walking.' Cissy followed her mentor.

'Will they be OK?' She asked Tess.

'Oh aye, they will now. I left them fast asleep; they'd sat and talked all night. They were for running away to sea. Take that look off yer face I talked them out of that. Told them a few tales to frighten them. I've promised to sort something out for them, so they'll stay put for now.'

'Thanks, Mrs Harvey, our Alice will be so thankful that they're OK, should let her know.?' Cissy was about to run back home with the news, but Tess stopped her by grabbing at the young girl's sleeve.

'No. If Alice stops worrying that father of yours will guess they've been found. I know it will be hard for her but it's for the best, trust me.'

Cissy looked up at Tess. She trusted this woman, but it was extremely hard to deny her sister the news that would come as such relief. Alice would be desperate to know that her young brothers were not in any more danger.

Tess sensed Cissy's concern. She took her by both arms and crouched down so that she was face to-face with Cissy. Softly now she said. 'Your Alice shows the emotion on her face. She would not be able to hide her relief from your dad and he would see in a moment. Can you see how he would get it out of her where they were?' Cissy nodded. 'If I thought, she would be able to hide it from him I would have told her last night when they first turned up. Let me get them away then you can tell her. OK.' Cissy nodded again and looked a little more comfortable with the situation.

❊ ❊ ❊

Geordie called to ask if the boys were home. He did not knock at the door before entering. This lack of courtesy always annoyed Alice; she seethed inside 'Treats the place like he owns it.' She thought when he just wandered in without knocking. On this visit, he walked in and sat at the table as if it was his natural right. He watched Alice for a few moments going about her business. She was up to her elbows in flour; she used her hands to push the loose strands of hair away from her face, smearing her cheek and hair with the white powder.

'Dad's still in bed and that's the best place for him. He needs to sleep that load off.' Alice informed the visitor with a very unfriendly voice. Geordie did not notice her animosity but continued to watch her put the bread into the oven. He looked on as she cleared the table of the flour-covered implements and gave Flo another bit of dough to pound into a grey stringy mess to match the now discarded piece.

'I'll 'ave a brew if there's one going, lass?' Geordie asked. She shrugged her shoulders and then went ahead to pour him tea into the cup with the handle. She poured in a little milk into his, but she drank hers black. There was no sugar to offer him. She sat at the table opposite Geordie, and they supped at the hot liquid. After a few minutes of silence, he spoke.

'Look, lass, about last night.' She did not look at him but continued to watch Flo play with the dough. 'Good God Alice look at me.' He raised his voice, and she turned her head sharply to look at him, but it was more of an angry glare. He raised his hands apologetically. 'Sorry, sorry. But I only wanted to help"

'Help?' she queried. 'What do you mean help?"

'With yer Da' She still looked confused, so he continued.

'Well with yer Da being angry last night about the lads. Sonny Porter had called him all sorts of things an....'

'Oh, I am sorry, was his pride hurt?' She interrupted him.

'Yer know what I mean. 'He needed to take it out on someone and.....' again she stopped him in mid-sentence.

'Oh aye. 'HE needed to come and take it out on us, or should I say, ME! 'n you came along for the entertainment.'

'No.' Geordie lowered his head. 'I followed him here after he'd slammed out.' Alice shook her head in exasperation and denial. 'He was angry.' Geordie continued. 'And I just thought I had better make sure he was all right.'

'He's all right, don't you worry.' Alice leaned towards the big fellow. 'He's always all right. If there is anyone in this house who's alright, it would be him; he sees to that himself.' She sat back in her seat and glowered at the man opposite.

'I've known your Da for a few years now and at heart 'es all right. He puts money on the table. Many a man would have left.' He nodded to where Nell sat smiling into the embers. Alice stared back at him in horror, her eyes wide and her mouth pulled tight.

'Well, that really goes to show that you know nothing about him or us, doesn't it?' She was on her feet now. 'Let me tell you, that man.' She spat out the words. 'That man left us years ago. Oh aye, he eats and sleeps here when he can stagger that far, but that's only out of habit or because no one else would have him. I don't know what he's told you but it's not her fault.' Alice indicated to her mother. 'He got her like that. I have seen her beaten till her face was swollen with bruises. Kicked her in the stomach till she'd lost babies cos he didn't want any more mouths to feed. 'Bout six I was when I first had to nurse her through what I now know was a miscarriage. And that's not all when he had finished with her, he turned my way. Oh aye, you need look shocked, but you must know how it was.' She pointed to Flo. 'Did he tell you about her 'n all, did he?'

'I presumed she was your sister.' Geordie's voice was quiet.

'Well, you presumed wrong.' She snapped back. 'My poor

mother could take no more, so she took to staying in bed. Oh! It didn't stop him; he still took his rights. I would cover my ears 'cos I couldn't stand to hear her screaming.' Alice was pacing the floor and waving her arms animating her tale. 'I must have been twelve. Aye, 'cos Harry was not a year old, and Mam had just had a stillborn, so yer see 1 was available.' She pointed to the room where her father lay asleep. 'He took me in there, and he hurt me over and over. Mind, that was just the start, he used me like he used to use Mam.' Geordie looked shocked at her words he could not believe that he was hearing this tale. Alice continued with her tirade.

'It only stopped after his 'accident', but you know all about that side, don't you? Did you think you were helping with that as well? I expect you thought we would benefit from that, did you? At least when he was getting what he wanted from me he threw a few coins on the table but that has stopped now and so has his money.' Her voice softened slightly, and she sat down at the table once more facing Geordie. 'Look around you. We didn't always live like this you know, we used to have nice things.' She pointed to the mantle. 'There used to be a lovely clock up there once. Mam's mother gave it to her, and we had some nice cups and things as well. He pawned the lot for his beer money. He slowly took everything from her including her mind, and when she lost that and stopped going out; he pawned her coat as well. He said she didn't need it anymore.' Geordie was looking around the room as she spoke. It saddened him to know the truth.

'I am so sorry lass.' Alice looked up at him.

'Are you? You've eaten well here, and you've taken him out, drank with him, took the food out of our mouths.'

'Aye! But I will make it up to yer, I swear I will.'

'No. You're like him.' She picked Flo up from the floor. 'I've got work. to do.' She walked out into the yard and sat Flo in a makeshift playpen. Geordie followed her and helped her to pull the old wringer away from the wall. The sheets had been soaking in the tub so now she needed to slosh them a little before wringing them. Geordie stood with his shoulder against the wall watching her work. The smallness of the yard seemed to emphasise his height.

'Alice, please believe me when I say that I'm sorry, 'cos I am.' He was very sincere.

'Huh, yer don't know yer born.' She hammered at the sheets.

'Oh, well, I could tell you a few things if you'd listen, but you wouldn't understand.'

'Wouldn't I?' she continued to work while he talked.

'How old are you, Alice?' He asked.

'I'll will be seventeen in two months, but I feel more like seventy right now"

'Well, you only look fourteen.'

'Not an innocent fourteen though eh.' She laughed at the wry joke.

'I'm not much older than you.' Alice stopped scrubbing at the sheets and turned to look at him. 'You don't believe me, do you?' She shrugged her shoulders. 'I've always been big, so people think I'm older than I really am. I've just turned twenty.' 'What has this got to do with me?' Alice was getting impatient with him now.

'Well, I ran away from home when I wasn't much older than those young lads. Da had put me in the pits when I was eight and I couldn't stand it. I had watched him coughing up blood and worn out at 35, I didn't want to end up like him'.

'Aren't the pits dark and narrow?' She asked.

'Aye. And damp and cold.' Alice turned and looked at him again.

'Then why did you help to send Eddie and George up chimneys? No difference as far as I can tell.' She went back to her washing, pushing and pulling at the heavy wash pole harder in her anger.

'I couldn't stop him. He was determined to get them into work.'

'If I remember right, it was your idea.' Water splashed out of the tub soaking her skirt.

It had been his idea, but he thought he was helping. Bert had said they needed work, and he knew where there was work going.

'I thought it would put some money your way.' Alice took a step away from the tub and placed her hands on her hips before answering him.

'I've not seen a penny of that money for months. Those lads were good little providers when they were here. Rabbits when they could catch 'em and pigeon too. I never asked 'em where they went or how they came about the odd vegetables that came our way. People might have thought they were running wild, but they could at least see daylight and stretch their legs. Can't do that up a chimney, can they?' Geordie shrugged his shoulders in defeat. Alice was thoughtful for a moment. 'There is something you can do if you really are sorry.' 'Anything,' Geordie replied eagerly.

'Stop dad from finding them.'

'That won't be difficult. He gave up last night after checking a couple of alehouses.'

'Of course he did.' Alice had lifted the sheets into the wash basket and was about to carry them the short distance to the mangle. Geordie rushed over to take the heavy burden from her and placed the basket by the old mangle. He turned at the sound of Bert's voice coming from the kitchen.

'Get out of the bleein' way woman.' Geordie smiled knowingly at Alice then went into the house to distract Bert from his wife.

* * *

Two days later Cissy was able to tell Alice the whereabouts of the two boys. Tess had sent them away to her sister who had married a farmer over the other side of the Cleveland hills. This was far enough away to keep them safe from their father's clutches. Tess had put the boys onto the cart and paid the driver to take them to the farm lane end. Eddie had repeated the instructions back to Tess word for word until he knew them by heart.

'Get off the cart at Ayton Beck Farm. Stay on the track and go straight to the second cottage and ask for Mrs Elsie Cooper then give her the note.' Tess had scribbled a brief note to her sister explaining the circumstances that the boys were in and asking her to find them work and shelter. So, with the note folded neatly in Eddie's pocket and bread and cheese wrapped up in a cloth in case they became hungry, the boys waved goodbye to the smoky industrial town and the life they had known.

The Allertons lost three boys that month, it was Joe who brought news of Albert. At Alice's request, he had gone to the pottery to enquire as to why Albert had not been coming home. The foreman informed Joe that Albert had not been to work for two months, and would Joe please inform Albert Allerton that the job was no longer his. A young boy directed Joe to a house down by the docks, he had seen Albert with a lass called Doris Withers.

A very obese man, dirty, sweaty and out of breath with the effort of the short walk to the door told Joe.

'Caught thieving on the docks he was. He's up before the courts next week. Silly sod. I told 'im to be bloody careful. Always took too many risks.' He chuckled with delight at Albert's misfortune, the fat wobbled around the huge frame. Joe was pleased to leave the vicinity of the smelly individual.

When Joe had finished telling Alice the tale, she simply shrugged her shoulder and continued to prepare the vegetables.

'Should we tell Dad?' Joe asked

'Why? We would only get the blame. Let him find out for himself.'

❋ ❋ ❋

Two weeks later Bert came home early and sober. He went into his room and stayed there all night. Some strange noises came from the room, but they all ignored Bert. Geordie had followed him into the house and told Alice about Albert's deportation. Bert had the news from an old workmate from his days on the docks.

'He is completely devastated,' Geordie told Alice. 'He got a few minutes with the lad before they took 'im down.' Alice shrugged her shoulders uncaringly. 'Don't you care at all Alice?' Geordie was surprised by her attitude.

'Not a lot.' She replied. 'I knew he'd been arrested two weeks ago, but there was nothing I could do then and there's nothing I can do now, save my tears for those who deserve them.'

SEVEN

It was a freezing morning in November, ice covered the inside of the grubby windows, and he could see every breath he took. His coughing produced huge clouds of exhaled vapour. To stay warm Bert had gone to bed fully clothed. His overcoat lay over the bed for extra warmth.

The room felt cold and lonely, now Albert had gone, and Joe had left. Their presence had offered a little comfort to a lonely man. Bert grieved for his lost son. The only one of them he had really cared for or had cared for him. There was nothing to keep him here now; he planned to leave as soon as he got his money together. He had done all right lately and had added to his nest egg. All his money had been too late to save his son Albert from the deportation order, but it would see him through quite a while.

Now that the nights were beginning to pull in and the sun no longer held any warmth he decided to go before the end of the year. As most men were migrating up to the Northeast for work in the budding steel industry, he would be heading south. Not in search of work, but to search for a more comfortable life.

'This is the last time I'm sleeping in this bed.' He thought to himself. He clambered from beneath the blankets and pulled the top pillow away. Under this was a bolster pillow with extra stuffing. He removed the first fist full of cotton stuffing from the pillow and then his fingers found the leather bag. With a self-satisfied smile, he sat on the bed and emptied the contents onto his overcoat. 'Quite a haul' He thought, his haul amounted to eleven sovereigns and loose change of four pounds, nine shilling and seven pence. He had surprised himself at being able to save so much.

He returned the coins to the bag, tossed it into the air then caught it, over and over like a child with a ball. As he did, so he thought over his plan to escape the drudgery that had been his life. With a sudden movement, he placed the bag under his pillow and dragged on his overcoat. He was about to leave the room when he looked down at the pillow; thoughtful for a moment he pursed his lips and frowned. He decided that the bag would be safe, and he left the room.

In the kitchen he found Alice scrubbing the table, the fire burned, and it was warmer than the freezing bedroom he had just left. His wife was at her usual place by the fire and Flo played happily with a couple of wooden spoons and a bundle of rags. He watched the scene for a moment. He was not going to miss them at all. None of them had ever cared for him and they had certainly not shown him any respect.

Only Albert the eldest had ever loved him and now he had gone. The sooner he got away from this dump the better. Alice stopped her scrubbing and looked up at her father as he slammed the door. She aimed a murmured obscenity at the hated individual who had just left and then resumed her work.

It was a long slow walk back from the market with Flo. The bag containing the few bruised and damaged potatoes and vegetables became heavier as Alice trundled towards home. The child was reluctant to walk, her feet were numb with cold. The crude leather shoes bit into her toes, with no stockings to ease the skins contact with the old ill-fitting footwear. Although she did not complain verbally, she pulled against her mother, distracted by the surrounding sights. A dog ran across their path and Flo wanted to run after it. She pulled against her mother's restraint.

'Oh Flo, please walk and don't tug.' Alice chastised the

child who never heard her words. Her deafness was a blessing in some respect. She never heard the angry raised voices and harsh words used at home. Both Alice and Cissy had noticed that the child did not speak but made grunting noises. 'She'll talk when she's ready.' Alice had said to Cissy. As she was a pleasant and quiet child, she was typically easy to cope with.

The mother and child neared the old cottage they called home. They walked down the narrow back lane and entered the yard. As Alice opened the scullery door, she heard her mother screaming. Shocked, she dropped the bag of vegetables and let go of the child's hands. Closing the yard door so that Flo would not get out she ran into the kitchen. There she saw her mother on her feet waiving the iron poker around her head and screaming over and over at her father. He stood red-faced on the opposite side of the table shouting and cursing at his wife.

Alice rushed over to her mother and tried to calm her. She managed to take the poker from her and gently lay it on the table out of her mother's reach. Bert was still shouting.

'The bitch was gonna kill me. You saw her.' With a shaking hand, he pointed to his daughter. 'Keep her away from me, do you hear?' He turned and went into his room.

'There, there.' Alice soothed Nell, stroking her hair as she spoke. 'He's gone, shush now.' She pacified her mother. Suddenly realising that she had left Flo in the yard she went to bring the child into the warmth. Flo was quite happily arranging the vegetables in rows. She had bitten into a potato and had decided that it was not very tasty so had invented a game instead. Alice had only been in the yard with Flo for a few seconds when she heard her father bellowing again. 'Oh God help me.' She thought. 'Not again.' This time she picked up Flo and carried her into the kitchen but quickly dropped her onto the mattress. Her father had picked up the poker from the table and was now waving it around threatening Nell.

'You took it didn't yer?' The iron bar caught Nell on the back. She lifted her arms to protect her face. The poker caught her again on the shoulder. 'That was mine, you bitch. Poking around where you shouldn't.'

Alice screamed at him to stop but he ignored her, intent on beating his wife with the iron bar. At first, Nell cowered away from the angry blows but then she found inner strength and began to fight back. She kicked and punched at her assailant.

Alice stood helpless, her hands covering her mouth that muffled her pleading for it to stop. Nell fought like a vixen until Bert got the better of her and punched her in the face and she fell to the floor. The back of her head hit the stone fire surround with a thud. He raised the poker and crashed it into the side of Nell's head, once, twice and then a third time. Nell lay motionless, blood pouring from her temple.

Alice screamed.

Suddenly Bert realised that his wife had stopped fighting, and he dropped the poker, with a clatter it hit the floor. He looked down at the prone figure and began to mutter unintelligibly. Alice rushed over to where her mother lay and cradled the bleeding head. Tears blinded her eyes as she looked up at Bert.

'You've killed her. She's dead. You've murdered her'. Bert shook his head denying his daughter's words.

'No. No l 'aven't.' But he could see that he had killed Nell. He started to babble again: this time Alice heard the words. 'She took me stuff. The silly, barmy bitch. She shouldn't 'ave been in my room. Haunted me for years she 'as. l saw 'er come out of there. I know she's taken it.' Alice wept and rocked her mother's lifeless body.

The tragic scene that Joe witnessed as he walked through the door at that moment, he would remember for the rest of his life. His mother's blood-covered head was cradled in Alice's arms. Alice crying uncontrollably and rocking the dead woman. Bert stood motionless looking down on them muttering with his arms hung loosely by his side. Flo had walked across to her mother and was tugging at Alice's sleeve for attention. Time froze as Joe watched the terrible spectacle. Bert turned around slowly and looked at Joe, he opened his mouth as if to speak, hesitated then spun around on his heels and ran into his room only to appear again seconds later with a large bundle. Without looking behind him Bert left the house through the front door, leaving the rest of his family.

* * *

The inquest into Nell's death had concluded that she had died at the hands of her husband who was now a fugitive. Alice sat quietly by the kitchen fire, staring blankly into the embers as her mother had for so many years. She had to pick up the pieces of the tragic affair. Stricken with grief and remorse she could only blame herself. Why had she left her mother alone? So often she had found someone to watch her while she had gone to the market. If only she had waited for Cissy to return home from the salon none of this might have happened.

Now she had to think of the future and try to put this terrible thing behind her. Cissy must go to Tess Harvey's. Tess has always wanted her to live over the road in her fine house. It was too big for one and Tess loved Cissy. She would ask her later to take her as soon as possible.

Joe had settled with his new job and lodgings, now he could make a new life for himself. She did not want to burden him with this household; he was too young to tie down so cruelly. Her own future and that of Flo were going to be a little more difficult to decide. Of course, she knew she could rely on Cissy and Joe for financial support until she could find a position somewhere. But where? What could she do?

Her life had always been in this place looking after the family. She had no training, and she would still have to care for Flo. She would never go to the Workhouse she would die first. There must be something that she could do. If she could get work, she might manage to pay the meagre rent and live simply, she had never worked outside of the house, but she was certain that she could get something.

She glanced across at where Flo sat playing quietly with a rag doll Cissy had fashioned out of spare rags. Who would care for her while she was working? As she pondered her fate, she heard someone enter. She looked up at the big frame of Geordie. He stood in the doorway tearing at his cap in awkward embarrassment.

'I don't know what to say, Alice.' He spoke quietly and emotionally. 'I thought I should see how you were. I don't suppose that there is anything I can do?' He was searching for the right thing to say and was finding her silence disturbing. 'I want to help Alice. I'd have come sooner but I didn't know how I stood.' Alice sighed and shook her head. 'I know I was yer Da's pal, well sort of, but I didn't think 'e could ever do what he did. I didn't know him that well really. 'E always kept his own council really. A dark horse 'e was. Never thought a scrawny little fella like him could do that.' Alice raised her hand to stop his babbling.

'You are talking as if it was him that is lying in his grave, not my Mam.' She was angry with him. 'The bastard killed my Mam and you come here like he just died a hero.' She turned back to the fire. 'Go away.'

'I'm sorry. I am not very good at this. I am trying to figure all this out in me head.' He pulled an old wooden packing case from under the table and sat facing her. 'Help me understand Alice.' He stretched out his hand to touch hers, but she pulled it away from him sharply. 'Please Alice.' She continued to stare into the fire. 'What are you going to do?' He asked her. She shook her head in reply. 'Then will you hear me out?'

Alice looked up at him. Her face was streaked with tears and her eyes red and swollen from the crying. Taking her silence as a cue to talk, he continued. 'You know that I have always cared for you, and I want to look after you. I don't have a lot, but I'll get a steady job 'n settle down. No more thieving or drinking. I'll come here and take care of you and little Flo.' He paused to look at her reaction, but she just stared at him blankly. 'You need a man about the place, and you'll soon get to know my ways. There is nothing to hold us back. I don't have to give any notice at my lodgings so I could move in straight away. I could come in as a lodger at first if you like.'

She still did not answer but her face was full of thought. Geordie leaned forward and took hold of her arms and said earnestly. 'Alice please let me look after you. You know it makes sense and I really care for you.' She stood up and shoved him away from her.

'I told you once before never to touch me and I meant it.' He stared up at her.

'Alice?' He pleaded with her.

'No. No!' She raised her voice. 'This is not what I want. I don't want you. I don't even want to stay here.' She swung around to face him. Pointing to the chair she had just vacated she continued. 'Do you think that I want to sit there like me mother, no way?' She laughed. 'Thank you, Geordie, thanks for helping me decide. 'Cos now I know that l can't stay here.'

'But Alice....' He stood up and walked towards her. She backed away from him. 'You need me; I'll even marry you. We will be a real family, you Flo and me. Few men would take both of you on, would they? Think about it. What will you do with Flo around your skirts?'

'Flo will come with me!' Her face was set in determination.

'Stay with me Alice, please.' But Alice resolved to leave, and he could see that there was nothing he could say that would change her mind. Defeated he picked up his cap from the table and went to the door. As he was about to open it, he turned to her again. 'Will you do one thing for me, Alice?' She did not reply but bent to pick up Flo who was showing signs that she needed the toilet. Geordie bent his head and shuffled his feet before continuing. 'Give me a couple of weeks to prove to you that I mean what I say. I am not like yer Da and someday I'll prove it. I'll show you that I can make a home for you and Flo, if not here then I'll find us another place.' He left the house slowly, hoping that she would call him back. Alice turned away and took Flo into the scullery without answering Geordie.

* * *

That night she was unable to sleep. Tess had willingly agreed to take Cissy, as she knew she would. Concern for her and Flo came from all quarters. Tess offered them a home and Joe had suggested they all move somewhere together, but Alice would have none of it. She wanted to leave this town and everything that had happened behind her. The question now was how.

The fire had burned low, so she had placed her mother's cape over her shoulders. It felt soft and warm against the night chill. When it was new, it must have been a very luxurious garment. Now it had shrunk and faded, and the stitching was breaking. Alice pulled the cape tight around her; memories of her mother flooded her thoughts, and she began to weep quietly once more.

As she wept, she stroked the fabric of the shawl and fingered the broken stitching. Somehow, she felt closer to her mother, she could feel her tortured mind and the shattered body of her. The smell of poor Nell still lingered on the garment. She could feel the comfort that her mother had craved and received from the worn-out cape. With a feeling of anger and despair, she took the cape from her shoulders and threw it onto the table where it landed with a clatter.

Surprised by the heavy fall of the cape Alice stood and went to investigate. The fasteners were mother-of-pearl but not heavy enough to have made such a noisy landing. On closer examination, she found small objects trapped somehow in the folds of the lining and a cleverly hidden pocket. Her fingers explored the pocket that had become threadbare with use. Caught on the threads was a rusty brass buckle. She remembered the day her mother had rushed into the house

68

with her 'treasure' after one of her walks.

Forcing the tear wider she plunged her hand deeper into the lining. Probing in between the quilted fabric she pulled out more treasure. Silver coins, a glass clasp and a length of tarnished fine chain. Astonishingly, she also found six gold sovereigns and four small silver spoons.

Alice spread the items out in front of her. These were her mother's treasures. Most of it was useless old trinkets and childish things, however, the coins and spoons were a gift from the grave. Now she could plan her escape from this awful room. She stopped for a moment to consider where the sovereigns had come from. Suddenly realising that she must have taken them from Bert's room, she would not have picked them up from the street. The spoons were the same as those Bert had thrown on the table when he had come home bleeding. Alice fingered the six sovereigns, was that all her mother's life was worth?

EIGHT

He hammered and banged at the door but there was no response. The cottage lay in darkness. On investigation of the rear of the building, he found the scullery door open. The pots and meagre belongings lay neatly on the yellowed paper-lined shelves. The kitchen where he had enjoyed greasy stews and her freshly made bread was just as he had left it two weeks previously. She had gone shopping he thought, so he sat patiently on the rickety chair by the cold lifeless fire.

A shiver went through his body as he awoke with a start. Darkness had fallen, and she had still not come back. He found pieces of kindling and discarded coal lumps in the backyard and lit a small fire in the grate. Three cigarettes later he knew she was not going to return. With a heavy heart, he lay on the lumpy shakedown bed in the corner of the room, and he slept. His dreams are entangled with images of Alice and Flo. Nell walked through his head singing children's songs and dancing. Then he was looking down on a field of ripened corn, a child was running through the golden sea. She was waving up at him, her hair flowing in the breeze. He drifted slowly down towards her, but she vanished then a haggard-faced old woman, who spat at him a fluid, which stung his eyes and blinded him.

After the darkness came intense heat, and the flickering flames licked at his feet as he ran down the dusty lane. As the flames were about to engulf him invisible hands wrapped a soft white blanket around him. He turned to see Alice smiling at him, her face covered with a widow's veil. He called her name as the child Flo dragged her mother from him. When he woke the sweat on his brow mingled with his tears as he cried for his lost love.

* * *

With money in her pocket, a bundle of her few possessions under her arm and Flo tottering behind Alice left her past behind her. She headed south towards York, a penny ride on the carrier cart as far as Thirsk shortened her journey by a day. The small market town did not offer her enough security. She needed anonymity which the small population could not offer, so after a night of rest, she continued to York.

The magnificent Minster towered over her, no matter where she walked the imposing building dominated the town. She meandered along the Shambles and in and out of the narrow ancient streets. The market closed for the day, and she had still not managed to find work.

Her three days at the boarding house and the meals she had taken were making a hole in her purse. Flo was winging behind her hungry again. The delicious smell of fresh pastry wafted down a very narrow cobbled alleyway. She realised that she was also feeling hungry, so she followed the delicious aroma.

Mrs Samuelson, a slender lady of middle years sat quietly in the corner of the pie shop knitting a pair of gloves for her husband. As the door opened, she looked up to greet the customer. The sight stole her heart in one moment. A little girl muffled up against the cold so that her round pink face shone out from an abundance of wool wrapped about her head and neck. Her shoulders were draped in a huge woollen scarf; the ends were brought to the front and crossed over then tied around her back. She looked as though she were wearing all her clothes at once.

The child beamed a smile and walked closer; her boots clumped on the wooden boards as her encumbering clothing impeded her movements. She held the gloved hand of another girl who was much older but dressed similarly. The older girl was pale with dark rings around her big brown eyes. The child broke free and walked over to the kind-faced woman. She stood just inches away from her and smiled so sweetly, the vision would have melted the coldest heart. The older girl called her back.

'Flo don't be rude. Come here.' The child did not respond. 'I'm sorry,' Alice said to the woman behind the counter. 'She's hungry.'

'Well then Flo, we had better find you something to eat.' Mrs Samuelson liked the look of this little angel. She held out her arms and Flo went to her without hesitation. 'I'm afraid that we are waiting for the evening pies to come out of the oven, but I just happen to have one here with a broken crust that I was saving for a poppet like you' She gave Flo the small meat pie and without further ado, the child sat on the floor and began to devour it.

Alice had removed her gloves and was proffering a few coppers.

'Oh, my dear, we do not pay for broken pies. Besides, it is my treat to the adorable child.' She leant forward and took Flo's woollen gloves off. 'Your big sister here looks like she might want a tasty pie too.'
Flo did not break her attention from the delicious pastry.

'Yes please.' Said Alice. 'Pie and peas with a little gravy would be lovely.' Again, she tried to give the woman the payment.

'As I said the evening pies will be awhile, but you may sit and wait.' Mrs Samuelson pointed to three chairs along the newly whitewashed wall. Alice sat down and watched Flo eating the pie. The silence is broken only by Flo's satisfied grunts until the proprietor spoke again. 'We usually have everything ready for the evening by now, but our assistant left us a week ago and left us shorthanded. My husband does what he can to help with the pastry, but he is better with the fillings.' Alice listened with interest to the woman's words.

'I am looking for work in the town, but I do not have any experience.' Her voice subdued and timid, she hardly dares to hope that she would get employment here.

'Really.' Replied Mrs Samuelson. A small overweight elderly man walked through to the shop. Alice presumed he had been in the kitchen. A huge apron smothered in flour completely covered his clothing

'Isaac this young lady is looking for work.' He shrugged his shoulders at the statement and then turned to Alice.

'Can you cook?' She nodded at the curt question.

'Only simple food Sir.'

'We only bake simple pies.' His voice tinkled with laughter. He looked down at the child on the floor his wife now crouched down cleaning the crumbs from Flo's pretty mouth. He knew at once why his wife was showing such interest in the skinny girl swathed in wool, she needed to care for a child and if he guessed right, these two would come as a pair.

After twenty years of marriage no babies had appeared, and the nursery his wife had prepared just after their marriage had remained empty. God was often cruel; his Sarah would have been a good mother, but it was not to be. He deliberated just for a second before he spoke again.

'The position would be live in, we start very early, and many late nights.' Alice nodded.

'I have done demanding work. My mother, who was invalid, relied on me to look after the family. She died recently and the others have found work and lodgings leaving just Flo and me' Alice prayed that she had said the right thing. She could happily work here; they seemed like two nice people and the atmosphere was warm and friendly. After a short silence, the woman spoke again to her husband.

'Tell her when to start dear.' He waved his arms in mock defeat.

'Can you begin tomorrow?' Alice nodded; she hardly dares to speak for fear of breaking the spell. 'Good. Bring what you need at seven and we will settle you in upstairs.' He went back to his pies. Mrs Samuelson spoke to Flo while slackening off her tight shawl.

'You had better take these off or you won't feel the benefit when you go outside.' She was stroking the long wavy hair. 'You and your sister will like being here. Of course, you will have to share a room, but it is a spacious room with a big bed.' Alice watched the woman fuss over Flo. Although she was pleased, they had found somewhere at last something ate at her happiness, but she was unsure what.

* * *

Geordie had asked everyone he could about the whereabouts of Alice and Flo. Neither Cissy nor Joe had any notion of where she had gone.

'All I know is she sent me over to stay with Mrs Harvey and she was going to look for work. She did not tell me or Joe where she was off to, but I know she took Flo with her 'cos she was seen getting on the cart with her.' Tess Harvey would not even speak to him, even if she had known.

His only option was to wait and see if she would contact Cissy when she settled, so he paid one more visit to Alice's younger sister at the salon. Tess Harvey sent him away with a flea in his ear before he managed to see Cissy, but he would not give up. One day I will be back he vowed. I will find her if it takes me years. He was not to realise just how long it would take him before he returned to the cottage.

74

NINE

The sun streamed through the large picture window of the salon. Cissy crouched down at the feet of a rotund woman who would not stand still. She kept looking around to see the rear view of the gown making the pinning of the hem difficult.

'It's beautiful Miss Allerton. The colour is simply perfect.' She turned around again to where Cissy crouched. 'You have a talent you know.' Cissy smiled in answer.

'Yes, I have been told, but I must insist you stand still, or this hem will be crooked.' The woman stood still for a few moments but moved again when Miss Wrightson entered.

'I've just been telling your assistant how talented she is Miss Wrightson. You must agree with me, she is wonderful.'

'Yes, she is a real gem Mrs Pollock, we are incredibly lucky to have her. Now look at this charming hat, I believe it will go perfectly with that new gown.' She took the hat from Miss Wrightson and cooed over the feathers and trims. Cissy stood up from her awkward position grateful for the opportunity to allow life to rush into her toes.

'Be careful about how you move Mrs Pollack, there are a lot of pins in there.'

'Oh, thank you, Miss Allerton.' Miss Wrightson and the customer moved nearer to the long mirror to view the outfit. 'Would you make some tea dear?' Miss Wrightson asked Cissy.

Taking her cue to leave, Cissy went into the backroom to brew tea for the customer.

Tess Harvey sat at the large table stitching a heavy brocade bodice. She was getting on in years and her eyesight was beginning to fade, so she kept holding the garment away from her large chest to check if her stitching. Although her fingers were still nimble, they were misshapen with arthritis and were often so painful she was unable to work. No matter how slow she was, Miss Wrightson kept her in work as she so rightly stated.

'The place would not be the same without dear Tess,' Cissy asked her friend if she would like a cup of tea.

'Yes, dear! Have you ever known me to refuse? Don't use the best china on me though. Save that for whomever Miss Wrightson is fussing over'. She put her work aside. 'Come and sit by me Cissy and let us have a bit of a chat. You've been so busy today; I've hardly seen you'.

Cissy sat by her companion.
'How are the lessons coming along?' Tess asked Cissy.

'Oh, very well.' Cissy was learning to play the pianoforte. She had attended the mission school for over six years and is now considered to be an educated young lady. She had been a model student, and Tess was enormously proud of her ward.

'And how is Mathew?' Cissy blushed slightly at the mention of her music teacher's name, and this did not go unnoticed. Tess pulled a face and nudged the young woman gently.

'He's very well, thank you.' Mathew was the minister's son, and he was also the main reason that Cissy had been so keen to attend school for the past year. When he had offered her music lessons, she had eagerly agreed. Mathew was a mild-mannered gentleman, five years older than Cissy. He had recently gained a position as an assistant teacher in the new 'Academy for Young Gentlemen'. This was a great achievement and would enhance his career. The 'Academy' was an imposing building recently built on the edge of the town. The students were aged between six years and fourteen. Some attended as day students, but the majority were boarders as the families lived as far as York. Tess believed that Mathew wished to court Cissy, however, the two youngsters needed a push, as they were both as shy and awkward as two fledgelings.

'Why don't you invite him to tea?' Cissy looked up at Tess in feigned surprise.

'Oh. I don't think he would. He's terribly busy.' She blushed again.

'Don't be daft, ask him to come on Saturday. If you don't, then I will.' Cissy knew that there was no point in arguing with Tess, so she nodded.

'All right I will ask but don't be disappointed if he is unable to come.' Tess smiled and thought 'Well that's a start.' A voice called from the main salon requesting the assistance of Cissy, putting an end to any further discussion about the shy tutor.

❈ ❈ ❈

Tess had insisted, that the best china should be set on a table in the small modestly furnished sitting room. Unlike Cissy's old house over the road, Tess's home was modern and had two bedrooms upstairs and two rooms downstairs with a good-sized scullery attached. It was as neat as a new pin and Cissy was so proud to be living there. She was in the kitchen putting a few finishing touches to the tea. The crustless small, mouth sized sandwiches sat neatly on pretty doilies on each plate. Mathew had never visited her home before, and she was incredibly nervous.

She looked out of the window at her old home across the road and felt ashamed that she had thought Tess's home unsuitable. In comparison to the hovel opposite this house was a palace, and she should be incredibly grateful to be residing here. She bit her lip as she remembered the inside of that dreadful place and its sad history.

The story of her mother's murder had been in the newspapers. Tess had cut out the items and put them in between the pages of a large bible. It had sounded strange to her when Tess had read out the words.

Under the headline 'Woman Brutally Beaten,' it read.

'Helen Alicia Allerton age 35 years was brutally beaten to death in her home. Her daughter Alice Allerton age 17 years witnessed the murder. Police are searching for Albert Allerton, the murdered woman's husband, in connection with the crime.'

The article went on to describe how he had committed the crime and a description of Bert circulated but he did not face justice. When Cissy had learnt to read, she read the newspaper cuttings herself. 'Helen Alicia,' she had repeated her mother's name over and over in her head. She had not known that her mother had such a lovely name. It was a sensitive, ladies name. Cissy built a picture of her mother in her mind around the name, blotting out the truth. Seeing only 'Helen Alicia' the elegant lady, sensitive and loving, not Nell the tired worn-out soul.

She came back to the present with a start at the sound of a knock at the front door. Quickly she removed her apron and went to open the door.

The afternoon tea went very well, and Mathew spoke kindly of Cissy's culinary efforts. Tess had stressed that it was all Cissy's work. 'Bakes a lovely sponge.' She had remarked, causing Cissy to blush deeply. Mathew, being a gentleman, had agreed that the tea was excellent. Once the meal was over and the polite conversation had come to a natural pause Tess made her excuses and left the two young people alone.

'Now you remain here and amuse our visitor Cissy whilst I busy myself in the kitchen.' Tess was already on her feet and collecting the dishes onto a large tray.

Now she was alone with Mathew, Cissy felt a little embarrassed. This was the first time that she had been alone with him. During lessons at the mission, there had always been two or three other people in the room with them. They sat in companionable silence for a few tense moments. Mathew watched her face intently. He saw the faint flush in her cheeks and the dark eyelashes flutter in sweet innocent awkwardness. She was gently stroking her lips with the tip of her tongue, not seductively but nervously as if tasting a sweet fruit for the first time. Mathew spoke first.

'I find your friend Mrs Harvey just as you described her. As you suggested I would think her truly kind and a good woman.'

'She's the kindest, most gentle person I know.' Cissy's love for Tess showed in every inch of her being. 'I don't know what l would have done without her, but I do know that if she had not taken me in, I would have been destined for a quite different life.' Mathew knew some of Cissy's history, but she had never spoken of it until now. He had read the newspapers and listened to the stories; however, this lovely creature still fascinated him. He took hold of her slender hand.

'I must thank her for allowing you to come to school. You know Cissy that I love you?' She lowered her head, not knowing how to reply. 'Had you not guessed?' he asked. Her head still lowered she gently shook her head and quietly said.

'Could you love me? You know who I am and... well, you know.' She stammered.

'I know that you are Cecelia Allerton, seamstress and ward of Mrs Theresa Harvey. You were a good student at school and now making your way in the world as a Christian hearted young lady.' He paused for breath then continued. 'Please, will you marry me?' The question came as a shock to Cissy and her mouth fell agape slightly and she was not able to answer him. Mathew knelt in front of her and gently held both her hands. Her eyes were wide in wonderment, the dark pupils enhancing the deep brown irises. 'Have I shocked you, my love?' His voice was quiet and caring. She nodded in reply. 'I must give you time

I know. I will speak to Mrs Harvey as soon as you wish. My post at the school is secure and I do have the means to look after you. Oh! Cissy, please let me have an answer soon.' He kissed her hand before returning to his seat.

Tess Harvey stumbled back into the room as Mathew returned to his seat. She noticed Cissy's amazed expression immediately. Being very astute she guessed that Mathew had made his feeling known and not wishing to interrupt the course of young love she suggested they all went for walk in the spring sunshine.

'May is such a lovely month. Don't you think so Cissy? Tess said to her young ward. 'An early evening walk will do us all good.'

The young couple walked slightly ahead of Tess until they reached the small park in the centre of the town. The park consisted of an oblong-shaped stretch of land donated to the public by a local dignitary. There were roses bushes planted in the centre and spring bulbs and flowers were in full bloom around about them. The trees were laden with 'May blossom' and the pink confetti-like petals lay scattered around their feet. To walk around the whole circumference of the park would only take ten minutes if at a slow pace. Placed around the edge were new wooden benches, each with a plaque of the generous patron who had donated a seat, placed at discreet intervals to afford a little privacy. Tess sat at the first bench and urged the two youngsters to continue their walk whilst she rested.

'I believe Mrs Harvey may have guessed that I have spoken and made my feelings known to you,' Mathew whispered to Cissy.

'Did you really mean what you said?' She asked him. He stopped walking and turned to face her. He placed his hands upon her shoulder and said sincerely.

'Yes, my love. I truly wish to marry you.'

'Then my answer would be, yes.' She smiled up at him, his face was a picture of boyish delight. He kissed her gently and demurely on the cheek then they continued their walk hand in hand. As they approached the place where Tess sat resting it was obvious to all around that the couple were very much in love. The afternoon had gone just as Tess Harvey had planned.

* * *

They planned for a wedding the following August. Giving them over a year to make their plans. The time leading up to this would be remarkably busy for Tess and Cissy as they fashioned a wonderful dress for the occasion. One thing impeded Cissy's complete happiness, she was desperately unhappy to leave her friend and mentor. It would be strange not to be with Tess and as she was getting older, she depended on Cissy for a lot more than she would admit. How would she cope when Cissy was not there to read to or chat to? It would be very lonely in the evenings for her. When she had discussed this with her Tess had insisted that she would be all right.

'I was used to my own company before.' She had stressed. So rather than upset her friend she smiled sweetly and promised that she would be a constant visitor.

The young couple would be living with Mathew's parents at the 'Manse'. It was a large house built close to the mission and if Mathew were to continue with his work there, he would need to be close to the school.

* * *

One cold windy afternoon in March Cissy sat in the warm cosy sitting room with Tess. They both stitched at their embroidery in quiet companionship. Without looking up from her work Tess said.

'We will have to get word to Alice about your marriage to Mathew.' Cissy nodded. 'I have already penned a letter to her, Joe will take it to Mr Cohen at the Synagogue when he is next off shift.'

When Alice left the area shortly after her mother's death, taking Flo with her, no one had known where she had gone. Then a year after her disappearance a strange-looking gentleman arrived on Tess Harvey's doorstep. Dressed all in black as if in mourning, on his head he wore a strange black hat and his hair fell in long curly locks at the side of his face. He introduced himself as Rabbi Cohen and explained that a friend and fellow Jew in Northallerton had news of a friend.

As he sat in Tess Harvey's sitting room drinking tea Tess read the letter he had delivered.

> *To my Dear friend,*
>
> *My kind employer has offered to write this letter for me. I hope it finds you, and Cissy well. I have been fortunate to find both work and lodgings with Mr Samuelson. He is a baker of a fine reputation and I assist him and his wife in their business. Flo and I are well and happy. If you wish to contact me you may speak to the kind gentleman, Mr Cohen who has kindly volunteered to act as a courier.*
>
> *Please inform Cissy and Joe that we are both in good health although a surgeon has attended to Flo and confirmed that she is deaf and dumb. However, she is happy and able to communicate with us in other ways. Thank you once again for your generosity towards Cissy. I remain your dear friend Alice.*

Alice had made a cross next to her name. The Rabbi took the word back to Alice advising that all was well. He became a frequent visitor to Victoria Terrace, as he needed to travel between Synagogues and would often call with news from Alice. Twice a year the sisters would correspond and once they had learnt their letters they would write more often.

A heavy knocking at the front door shattered the silence of the sitting room. Cissy carefully laid her work to one side and went to answer. Her brother Joe had grown into a fine sturdy young man, broad across the shoulders and strong muscular arms. He had courted and married Agnes from the sewing room and now they had a son Edward, who promised to grow into the image of Joe. It was never a surprise to see Joe on the doorstep, as he was a frequent visitor. He took off his cap and stepped over the threshold into the sitting room. Standing with his back to the fire warming his legs he spoke when Cissy had returned to her seat.

'I've had some news about Alice. Well, not her but of her employer Mr Samuelson.' He paused.

'Go on Joe. What is it?' Urged Cissy. She could see that Joe looked worried.

'I met Mr Cohen in town, and he said there was sad news. Mr Samuelson had taken ill with his heart and died.' The heat began to penetrate the cloth of his trousers and burn his skin, he moved away from the fire slightly as he continued. 'Apparently, the Missus is in a terrible state so has gone to live with her sister.'

'What has happened to Alice then?' Queried Cissy. She was frightened for her sister. 'Where is she? Has she sent a letter?' She was in tears at the thought of her sister and Flo back on the streets.

'All I know is that the business is to be sold and Alice will have to move on. Mr Cohen will be calling with the news I expect. He told me he was trying to find them both another position.' He shrugged his shoulders as he spoke. 'Alice will be all right. That Rabbi will see to that, I'm sure.' Joe declined the offer to stay for some tea. 'I've just come off shift and I haven't been home yet. Agnes will blow her top if I am too late.' He reluctantly left the warmth of the fire and went home to his wife and child.

✳ ✳ ✳

It was two weeks before they heard any news from Alice. Rabbi Cohen called and over a very pleasant afternoon tea, he explained the circumstances that Alice had found herself in.

'I have found a position for her as an assistant cook. In my travels, I get to know a lot of people and a friend of mine has a son called Joshua who works as a footman at High Fell House near Ayton. It is only about a day's walk from here. He told me of the vacancy for an assistant cook and I spoke to the butler there who kindly took Flo on as a kitchen maid as well. She is a bright child despite her impediment'

'You have been exceedingly kind to Alice and Flo for which we must thank You,' Cissy said.

'It is my pleasure, Miss Allerton. Your sister is a good woman. Now I must take my leave.' He took the letter that Cissy had offered. 'I will be certain to pass on your letter and wish you good fortune in your marriage.' He bowed his head slightly in salute and left. Tess watched as he walked away from the house. 'I think Mr Cohen has a soft spot for Alice.' She said to Cissy as she re-entered the room. 'He's very handsome. Do you think he is a little infatuated with her?'

'Stop that, Tess Harvey.' Cissy wagged her finger at the older woman. 'Anyway, it is known that they only marry their own faith so stop matchmaking.'
'Shame.' Tess began to clear away the tea plates noisily. Now that Alice and Flo were settled, Cissy fussed about the wedding. The big day was only a few months away and there was still the matter of leaving Tess to come to terms with.

Cissy loved Mathew wholeheartedly and his parents were very dear people. But how would she feel living with them? The Manse was a large house, larger than she had lived in before, the thought remained that it might never feel like home.

❋ ❋ ❋

Spring arrived late and May had started very cold, only a few weak rays of sun fell on the spring flowers. Tess had caught influenza and suffered terribly. It was the first days of June before she began to recover. After over two weeks in bed, she was now delighted to be in her sitting room where she was able to watch the world go by her window. Cissy had gone to work as usual but had left Martha, one of the neighbour's young daughters to look after the invalid.

Martha was only fifteen, but she was a sensible girl and a good nurse. She had brought her some beef broth and fresh bread.

'Me Mam made this for you Mrs Harvey, it's good 'n hot.' She placed the tray on the side table while she plumped up the cushion behind Tess's head. 'It's a lovely day outside; the sun has really come to stay now. If you feel up to it, we could take a short walk, stretch your legs a bit eh!'

Happy that her patient was now comfortable Martha placed the tray across her lap. Tess smiled weakly at her nurse and began to sip at the broth.

'That's right, now you eat that up while I just pop out and hang out the washing.' Martha left the room leaving Tess to eat the broth and stare out of the window.

The broth was as tasty as Martha had promised. She placed the bowl on the side table and sat back contented in the chair. From this window, she was able to see Cissy's old home. It had never been a very picturesque building, and now due to further neglect and lack of occupancy, it was decaying further. She thought back to those turbulent days when Cissy was a child.

Her lovely Cissy dressed in rags and half-starved most of the time. Playing out in the street barefoot and filthy, hair matted with lack of washing and brushing. 'Poor Nell', She thought 'Poor, poor Nell.' Her memories brought tears to her eyes and a lump in her throat. Now Cissy was to be a bride, she would marry her gentleman and live happily away from all that squalor. If only Nell had lived long enough to see how her brood had grown.

In only a few short weeks she would watch Cissy walk down the aisle with her young man. Mathew would be a good husband. She closed her eyes as she thought of the children that would come. A contented smile played across her face as she envisioned little copies of Cissy and Mathew rushing through the door shouting her name. Happy, laughing, clean children, well fed and well mannered.

As she sat dreaming, she felt lifted on a soft cushion, she was floating yet her head felt heavy, and her eyes would not open. Her head began to fill with the sound of rushing water over a rocky riverbed and the drum of her heartbeat pounded through her ears echoing back through the dark tunnel she was looking down. She was unable to move it was as if some heavyweight held down her arms.

Her eyes opened momentarily, and a red cloud swept across the window as she fell into unconsciousness.

Martha stood on the doorstep flapping her arms and speaking so fast that Cissy could not understand a word.

'Slow down Martha, you're not making any sense.' She pushed past the agitated girl and rushed into the sitting room. The words 'Mrs, Harvey' 'can't wake' and 'doctor' reached Cissy's ears, but they did not register until she saw the prostrate figure of Tess slumped in the chair. Tess's head hung to one side and the inert limbs hung lifeless.

Cissy rushed across to her and took hold of the limp hand. It felt cool but when she gently touched the sleeping woman's cheek there was some warmth. Cissy was immediately relieved that the woman was not dead. At that moment the doctor entered the room. Martha stood weeping and tearing at her apron. She was babbling between sobs.

'I only went out to hang the washing. I was only gone a few minutes.' The doctor completed his examination quickly.

'We will have to get her up to bed.' He turned to Cissy. 'Can you get a couple of strong men to help carry her upstairs?' Cissy nodded and then instructed Martha to fetch her brothers to help. The young maid wiped her damp face with the hem of her apron and left to find Freddie and Jack. Left alone the doctor explained that Tess had suffered a stroke.

'Quite a bad one, I think. We will know more in a day or

so. Get her up to her bed and make her comfortable. I will call and see her tomorrow.' Cissy remained cool and calm until Tess settled into her bed. Once she knew that there was no more, she could do for her dear friend she sat in the kitchen drinking a strong cup of tea.

She wept for her companion, blaming herself for not being at home with her. Poor Tess had been alone when this awful thing had happened. She swore that she would never leave her alone again. She owed everything to this woman. If not for her she might have ended up in the workhouse.

* * *

Mathew had been very understanding about the postponement of the wedding. Once Tess began to show some improvement, they would be able to reset the date. The young couple were taking a rare outing to the public park. Cissy had left Martha to watch the patient who was improving every day but was still very weak and paralysed down her left side. Her speech was very slurred and slow, but she was trying extremely hard to improve. Cissy knew that her friend had been incredibly lucky to survive a stroke of such magnitude. The doctor was amazed at his patient's progress.

'I really can't stay out too long Mathew.' She was very worried about leaving her dear friend.

'I know my dear, but I have important news.' He led Cissy to a vacant bench. 'Let us sit here for a while.' He brushed the seat with his hand to be sure that she sat on a clean area. They sat close, and he took hold of her hand. 'How is Tess really coming along?' He asked nervously.

'As you saw Mathew, she is doing quite well considering the severity of the stroke. But it will be a long time before she will be well, if ever.' She looked at Mathew's face. He was looking quite grim and anxious which was quite unusual as he was always of a pleasant disposition. 'What is wrong Mathew?' He looked away from her and watched a pigeon stabbing at a piece of stale bread.

'I have been offered a post which I am reluctant to refuse.' A group of starlings crowded around the pigeon's meal. 'A colleague of my father is taking a group of Missionaries to India, and he has asked me to join them.'

'I don't understand Mathew. Are you saying that you are considering going to India?' A small boy ran at the birds, and they flew away in a flurry of flapping wings. Mathew flinched slightly as one of the birds flew in his direction. He turned back to face his fiancé.

'My love I just wish us to be married as soon as possible and then we can go to India. There will be a need for teachers such as us.'

'But you have a position here. You don't need to go.' Cissy was frightened. 'I can't go to India. I'm needed here. Tess needs me.'

'I know how much you think of Tess, but this is especially important to me. I have always dreamed of a chance like this. Ever since I was a child and my father told me of the faraway places that Missionaries took the word of our Lord, I have wanted to see them for myself. I need to do this Cissy. Please say you will come with me.' Her face was stricken with grief. She was about to lose the man she loved because of her devotion to her dear friend and guardian.

'I can't leave Tess. She needs me now more than ever.' Mathew was aware of her misgivings and so he pleaded with her further.

'Tess would not expect you to stay with her forever. She knew that you were to be married and move out anyway. Her illness should not make such a difference. Martha is a good nurse, and she will take care of her very well. We will only be away for two years at the most'

'No Mathew! I cannot leave her with Martha. She needs me.' Cissy was beginning to cry. 'I will stay with Tess. I owe her everything. You must follow your heart.' The tears rolled down her cheek. The choice was apart tearing her apart. Her love for Mathew was profound but her dedication to Tess went deeper.

'Oh, my love, please come with me.' He begged her but she hung her head in sorrow.

TEN

The field was full of ripened corn undulated in the early autumn breeze. The sunset lit up the distant sky with glowing orange embers among high sparse clouds. It was a beautiful evening and a view that Eddie could never tire of watching. He and his brother sat together on the hillside watching the sun sink into the sea of yellow corn.

They had arrived at Ayton Beck Farm as two scrawny, half-starved urchins. Decent food, fresh air and demanding work seasoned the thin, undernourished bodies into strong healthy young men. Now they sat in companionable silence on the hillside. The day's work was over, and they were free to roam the hills and enjoy the surrounding beauty.

The time the two boys had spent working for Sonny Parker had taught them to appreciate the fresh air and freedom the farm brought. When Tess Harvey had bundled them into the cart with pockets full of food and a note for her sister, she had opened a whole new way of life for the sad youngsters.

Tess's sister, Elsie, had been surprised to open the cottage door and find two small, dusty lads on her doorstep. Young George had cried all the way. His grimy face was smeared with the black tramlines of tears, wiped with his shirtsleeve. Both were still bruised and bewildered after their escape from the cruel chimney sweep.

After a hot meal and two days of tender loving care

from Elsie, the lads recovered enough to do small chores for the farmer. They lodged in the hayloft and soon settled into a routine. They were so grateful for the kindness shown to them that they worked hard. The country air and demanding work furnished them with huge appetites and Elsie supplied them with huge meals to match. She loved to watch the youngsters eat. Her biggest regret in her otherwise happy life was the lack of sons. Her only daughter Elizabeth was treasured more so after James Robert had died as an infant. Unfortunately, they had not been any more children.

Eddie and George filled an emptiness in her heart and for this, she would always love them. Her husband was aware of her fondness for the boys and would not deny her the comfort she gained from looking after them. He treated them with kindness but worked them hard, and the boys in return loved the missus and respected the Boss.

Once the sun had gone down the two brothers gathered their tools and began the long walk home for supper. Eddie was nineteen and had grown tall. He stood as high as the kitchen door in the cottage and had to dip his when he entered or gain a lump on his head. He was thin like his father, but his limbs were muscular and strong from the farm work. Eddie was handsome, his dark, almost black hair grew straight. He wore it long, cut just above his shoulders and wore a flat cap to keep it out of his eyes whilst working. He always took the lead in everything the boys did, but they were still inseparable.

George had not kept up with his brother in height, like Joe his older brother, he was short in stature, and he had the same shock of unruly hair. He was quiet and undemanding, happy to follow in his brother's wake.

'Will you marry Elizabeth?' George asked his brother.

'Aye.' Eddie answered without altering his stride. George knew his brother was in love with Elizabeth, he was also quite aware that most of the girls they knew were in love with Eddie.

George, Eddie and Elizabeth grew up together. They had been inseparable as children. George had always looked at

Elizabeth as a surrogate sister, but it was obvious that Eddie was smitten with her right from the moment they had first met.

The two young farm labourers walked another mile before George spoke again.

'That Annie Jordan from over Ayton might not be pleased with you marrying Lizzie.' His boyish grin was infectious and soon they were laughing at their private joke.

Mr Cooper looked across the table at Eddie. The breakfast dishes still lay on the table in front of them.

'I'd like you to come into Stokesley with me today son.' Eddie nodded his agreement but was a little taken aback as his boss usually went to market alone. They only sent in a few sacks of potatoes and the vegetables harvested from the modest garden. It was not normally a job for two men. George nudged his brother secretly under the table. It was obvious to him that the boss wanted to talk to Eddie in private. Eddie kicked his brother's shin in retaliation to the suggestive nudge.

The two men climbed onto the loaded flat cart. Eddie looked down at George daring him to make an inane remark about the unpredicted trip.

'I'm going to sit with Ally.' George's favourite collie was in whelp with her first litter, he was anxious for her. He waved goodbye to Eddie and marched quickly into the barn where the black and white dog lay panting in pain.

Eddie and Mr Cooper set off on their short journey, waving farewell to the two women. Once out of sight of the farm Mr Cooper slowed the horse to a slow walk.

'Be nice to get away for a while. Eh.' He talked as if they were on a Sunday outing. Eddie just nodded. 'Yer don't say much do yer?' The lad shrugged his shoulders, dumb with embarrassment. 'I hope yer can find more to say to our Elizabeth or she'll soon get fed up wiv yer.' He chuckled and shook his head. 'I am right in thinking you are wanting to walk out with my daughter?' He twisted in his seat to see the young man's reaction to the question. Eddie's face held a grin that almost split his face from ear to ear and he was blushing a deep scarlet. 'Aye. I thought so.' Mr Cooper nudged his young companion. 'Go on ask me!' He demanded. Eddie pulled an embarrassing face before blurting out the words.

'I'd like to marry your daughter Sir.' Mr Cooper laughed loudly, and poor Eddie was unsure whether he should laugh with him or get upset at the outburst, so he chewed at his fingers instead. Seriously now Mr Cooper looked at the young man next to him.

'Do you love her?'

'Aye... I mean yes Sir.'

'Will you stay on the farm?'

'Oh Aye. We wouldn't want to move away.'

'And George?'

'He doesn't want to get married,' Eddie answered.

'No! What I mean is that you two are so close, what will he do?'

'Nothing.'

'What do you mean 'Nothing'? He'll have to do something. Will he stay on or what?'

'We just go on like before.' Eddie was completely dumbfounded. He did not understand how getting married would affect his brother. They had always been together, and nothing would ever alter that.

'Right.' Said Mr Cooper nodding his head in an exaggerated fashion. 'Lad, you really are something else.' He laughed again and then pulled off Eddie's cap and playfully slapped him on the head with it. 'We'll have to do something with that hair of yours if you're going to be a family.' He put the cap back on the lad's head back to front and pulled it down tightly. Still laughing he shook the reins to hurry the horse. 'Tell yer what; we'll get you a haircut 'n a good close shave. Surprise the women. Aye, surprise the cattle too. Milk yield might go up.' They now laughed together.

All the errands completed, and the cart parked up Mr

Cooper took Eddie into the barbershop. They both had a shave, and the barber took great delight in cutting the dark locks of hair from Eddie's head. The hair was still longer than most men would wear, yet somehow the cut emphasised his boyishly handsome face. The hair appeared thicker and wavier. His future father-in-law was amazed at the transformation.

Once a month it was Mr Cooper's general habit to meet his friends for a pint of ale and a chat. The two men crossed through the market to reach the 'Plough Inn' and as they walked through the crowded stalls to the Inn Eddie noticed a petite woman with dark hair. He stopped to watch her; his brow furrowed as he tried to remember where he had seen her before. She was walking away from a stall crammed with ribbon then she became swallowed by the crowd. Mr Cooper turned to see why his companion had stopped.

'I thought I'd seen someone I used to know.' He explained. The advantage of being taller than his boss meant that he could see further, but he still lost sight of the woman. 'She looked like my mother.'

'   No lad yer mothers de........down Middlesbrough'. He pulled at the lad's arm to urge him towards the Inn. He knew the boy's mother had died but he and Mrs Cooper had decided that it was best not to tell Eddie and George. They had been young when it had happened. They had gone through enough; Elsie had said, and the subject had not risen again.

Stokesley marketplace did not seem to be the place to enlighten this young man of his mother's demise. 'Come on son my throat's parched, for a pint. It must have been all that dust from your curly locks hitting the floor.'

The farmer wanted to show Eddie off to his cronies and fellow farmers, but Eddie declined. Something about the smoke-filled, stale smell of the place made his stomach churn. A dark memory stirred in him as he stepped over the threshold, so he made an excuse to leave, preferring to go for a walk. The older man was a little disappointed but was not one who pressed another into going against his nature.

Eddie explored the small market town. He had once passed through on the cart, on a wet and cloudy day. The place had not looked as cheerful or full of life as it did today. The small stream which flowed through the farm as well as giving it its name meandered slower and deeper behind the 'Plough' and on through the village. Eddie walked towards the sound of the running water and stood on the stone bridge to watch the ducks and geese fighting for the crumbs thrown to them. The cooler autumn sun still felt good on the back of his bare neck. People littered the banks of the stream, idly watching the fowl; others sat on the bank and ate bread and cheese, or warm pies purchased from the pie shop close by.

The beauty of the scene astounded Eddie. He always imagined that the towns, villages, or any built-up area would be like the dirty, crowded, smoke-ridden hovels around the docks. The sweep had dragged him all over both sides of the dirty river Tees and pushed him up the chimneys of huge houses considered to be 'out of town, but he had never seen a place as wonderful as this. Tidy, well-kept gardens and clean cobbles. The widows of the neat cottages sparkled in the sun reflecting the peace and tranquillity of the whole place. As he pondered the scene and smiled at the antics of the birds fighting over a piecrust, he saw the woman again.

She was sitting alone a yard from the water's edge. To get a closer look, he crossed the bridge and casually walked towards her. He could easily continue along the river nonchalantly. He was about twenty yards from her when she stood up and brushed the grass from her skirts. Frightened in case he lost her again he quickened his pace. She turned to face him and began to walk towards the bridge. Closer now he recognised her.

'Alice!' He called out. She ignored him. Again, he called the name. She went to rush passed him looking fearful that he meant to harm her. Eddie stepped in her path and held out his arms as if to catch her. 'Alice! It is you, isn't it?'

'I'm sorry.' She stammered and shook her head. 'Please let me pass.'

'It's me, Eddie.' She looked up at his face still frightened and ready to flee. Eddie stepped back removed his cap and opened his arms wide. 'Don't you know your own baby brother?' She did not run away but looked at him again and with a cry of pure glee threw herself at him.

They hugged one another, and he swung her around. Anyone who passed by could feel the emotion of the meeting. People stopped to stare at the performance. One man almost fell into the river, while watching the scene. After the touching greeting, they walked to a nearby bench.

'I can't really believe that it's you, Eddie. The last time I saw you and George you were so small.'

'Aye, the country life agrees with me.' He hugged his sister again. 'Ee, Alice it is so good to see you.' They talked for a long time about their lives apart. Eddie told her all about the farm and the wonderful sunsets. She asked about George, and he told her of his engageme with to Elizabeth and his new haircut. He talked about the lambs in the snow and how he had learnt to milk a cow. Eventually, he ran out of words and Alice was able to update him on her own life.

'So, Flo is completely deaf?' He was genuinely concerned.

'Aye, the doctor said it was the fits. Mind those have stopped, she hasn't had a fit for years.' Alice bent her head and began to examine her hands.

'I think I should tell you about Mam. I don't suppose you know?' Eddie shook his head and frowned. Quietly she told him about how poor Nell died and that Bert was as far as she knew still running. Eddie shed a silent tear, not just for his mother but also for the pain and torment that Alice had suffered.

As the afternoon went by, they talked and caught up with each other's news. The sun was getting low as a short stocky man dressed smartly, his high shirt collar starched and a face to match approached the bench.

'Here you are, Alice. I have been looking for you all over the village. We were all to meet back at the cross in the market.' He sounded a little angry at having to come and find her. He was very well-spoken but with a slight Welsh accent.

'Oh, I am sorry Mr Evans. The time has flown by.' The smart Welshman glared at Eddie. 'May I introduce my brother Eddie?' Mr Evans was clearly relieved at the relationship and shook hands with the young man.

'I'm sorry to have to break up this happy reunion Alice, however, the trap is waiting to take us back to the house.' He bowed stiffly and indicated that they should begin to walk to the market square. Eddie walked with Alice and after promising to take George to see her at High Fell, they said their goodbyes and he made his way to the 'Plough'.

Mr Cooper was quite merry and talkative making it very awkward getting him onto the cart. He chatted and laughed, to himself, until he fell into an alcohol-induced sleep and snored loudly the rest of the journey.

Eddie and George visited Alice at the House as often as possible. Elsie Cooper had shown surprise that the boys were related to the new assistant cook at High Fell House.

'I met her once in Ayton. She doesn't look like either of you, does she?' She said to Eddie over the supper table.

'No, she is like our mother,' Eddie answered.

'It's a shame about the other sister.' Elsie had finished her meal and was waiting to clear the dishes away. The boys were unsure at first of whom she was talking about. 'The little deaf and dumb one.'

'Oh, you mean Flo.' Eddie exclaimed.

'Is that what they call her? She is a strange child. It is good of your Alice to look after her, really. The authorities could have put her away after the mother died.' She carried the dishes into the scullery. Eddie was not that surprised to hear Alice had kept the true parentage a secret, and he did not think that it was his place to correct the situation.

ELEVEN

The day had started out appalling and it seemed it would continue to worsen. He cursed the groom who had left the filly lame; she had been a gift from his mother two years ago for his twelfth birthday. He had been looking forward to his ride, so the news had not proved to calm him at all. The gravel crunched underfoot as he stormed down the drive after his sister. He had not meant to upset her and make her cry.

Now he would have to apologise for his crass behaviour. The school was bad enough, but the long holidays away from the place left him bored and restless.

He sat on the low wall separating the two levels of the rear gardens kicking idly at the loose gravel. Georgina was completely out of sight; the silly girl would be sulking somewhere before telling tales to Mama about the row. Bother and damn all women.

The movement behind the bush was slight, but he spotted the skirt lying low on the ground. Quietly he crept towards the row of Cypress trees that lined the garden wall. The figure crouched close to the whitewashed brickwork. It was not his prey but a smaller plumper girl. She did not notice his approach or turn when he coughed, so mischievously he lifted his well-booted foot and pushed the stooped girl off balance.
She toppled to one side with a cry of fright.

'What are you about my girl?' He shouted at the

frightened child. When she did not answer him, he knelt beside her and repeated the question louder and with more menace. She scrambled to her feet and pushed him aside almost trampling him as she made her escape. He fell onto the dry earth scraping his hand on the rough wall. It was then that he saw the drawings, drawn in coal and charcoal were three hunting dogs and a horse. They were primitive but had still captured the movement and grace of the animals. He was useless at art and could never control a pencil or brush, but he knew talent when he saw it. Muggy Minor, a school chum who considered himself the best artist in his form, was no match for the work in front of him now.

Higher on the wall he saw other sketches. He stood back to exam them from a better position. He knew the faces drawn there very well. Ugly caricatures of the staff. Mrs Ford, the cook, with her double chins and a large nose. Evans, the butler, with his sharp-pointed features drawn onto the body of a black rook. The child had captured Collins the head coachman's bulbous nose and crooked teeth so well that he could almost smell the halitosis. His curiosity rose, he would have to find out where this girl had come from. She had dressed as a servant and obviously knew the staff well so that was where he thought it best to begin his enquires. He needed to hide these pictures somehow from other more authoritative people such as his father or even worse the head gardener.

'I'm sorry if she disturbed you, Master David.' Evans fawned at the young Master. 'She is a kitchen maid and can be difficult to control due to her disability Sir.'

'Oh, what is wrong with the girl?' David tried not to sound too occupied with a mere servant.

'She's a deaf-mute Young Sir. Her older sister is an assistant to the Cook. I'll see to it that she does not stray into the main gardens again Sir.' He bowed stiffly in return for David's dismissal of him.

'Deaf, dumb and talented,' David muttered to the closed door. He turned his thoughts back to removing the evidence of her work.

Stealthily he crept behind the tall conifers and with a lump of coal stolen from the coal-scuttle, which stood by the large fireplace in the library he began to rub over the drawings. The bush moved, and he heard a footfall. He felt her presence but continued defacing her work. For a split-second Flo froze to the spot when she saw him ruining her pictures then she flew at him with a force far stronger than her small frame suggested. With tight fists, she beat at his back and kicked his legs.

'It's for your own good.' He fought against her blows trying not to hurt her and eventually succeeded and pushed her away. Pinning her arms to her side so tight that she could not hit him again he spoke to her slowly and clearly. 'Stop that and listen.' With each word, he jerked her small body until she calmed. She had limited lip-reading skills, but she understood his manner, so she stood still and glared at him with angry eyes and a hard-set mouth. 'Right, now I've got your attention. I mean you no harm.' His expression softened, and she responded by softening her own face but only slightly and was still ready to fight against the destroyer of her work.

'That's better.' He smiled reassuringly and nodded. Slowly he slackened his grip and removed his hands from her. He slowly raised his hands in a sign of submission in front of his chest. Still, with a furious expression, Flo crossed her arms in front of her and stood defiantly in front of him. Using signs learnt in a
Parlour game he tried to tell her that he would bring her a pencil and sketchbook. 'Come here tonight at bedtime.' He placed his cupped hands to his face like a pillow and repeated. 'Bedtime.' Then he held his palms together and opened them to sign for book and pretended to draw on the open palm of his left hand.' Book and a pencil for you.' He pointed to her. Her puzzled face told him that she was not finding this easy, so he repeated the actions. When eventually she nodded and smiled at him, he gave a huge grin in return, and she turned and disappeared.

He kept his promise and took her two small pencil stubs

and a sketchpad from the schoolroom where his sisters took lessons with their governess. She waited patiently for him behind the trees.

She looked small and vulnerable sitting with her back against the wall and her knees tucked up to her chin. When she saw the book in his hands, she jumped to her feet and the joy in her heart lit up her face. The book bent slightly under the pressure of her hold as she hugged it to her chest. Her delight shone from her when he gave her the gift. David bent towards her slightly as she reached up to kiss him on the cheek before she once more flew off leaving him to watch her cross the garden. Her long dark hair had escaped the confines of the cotton cap and blew wildly about her shoulders as she hurried away from him.

Leaving him proud that he could bring so much pleasure with such a small gift.

TWELVE

Cissy had finished making Tess comfortable for the night and went to light the oil lamp in the sitting room. She thought she might write again to Mathew. Over the eighteen months, He had been away in India she had only received a handful of letters. His letters of late had been very polite and informative but lacked the passion that he once had for her. Did he no longer love her? Had he met another? She desperately longedd for his return.

The lamp sprang into life with a warm glow and a pop. She carried it across to the desk to collect the paper. As she passed the window, a movement outside caught her eye. Standing for a moment to look across to the old cottage which she used to call home, she saw a dark figure move across the window. 'Tramps!' She thought. 'That would mean more destruction to the already ugly, derelict building.'

Every year the place fell into further decay. The property owner had died years ago, and no one was taking responsibility for the row of single-story buildings. The last family to live there had moved out two years ago, now only tramps and drunken vagrants occupied the place. She turned away from the window and sat to pen her letter to Mathew.

* * *

Charles Edward Bingham stood for an hour watching the cottage. He was anxious to discover the whereabouts of the Allerton family, especially Alice. When he had last seen her standing by her mother's graveside, she looked lost and forlorn. He had watched the funeral procession at a discrete distance. The small, depleted family walked behind the hearse. A concerned neighbour had anonymously paid the funeral costs. He would have willingly paid the costs if he thought Alice would accept it. Although he had always thought of himself as part of the Allerton family, Alice had made it quite plain that he was not.

His decision to sail for America had been impulsive, but it had been the best one he had made. He had only thought to stay away for a brief time, long enough to make a new life for himself and Alice. Unfortunately, it had taken him more than ten years. He had worked his passage across to the new world of dreams and promises on a slow cargo ship, stopping at every lonely and exotic island on the way.

Once on dry land, he used his brain and brawn to learn how to herd cattle, ride horses and sometimes fight men. Now he was back but Alice had gone, and he still had no idea how to find her. His only hope was the neighbour Tess Harvey, but he was unsure what kind of greeting he would get. He received a good tongue lashing the last time. If only the old lady understood his feelings for Alice.

He watched the lights flicker into life in the row of street windows. The row of cottages still lay in darkness. After examining the rear of the row of low-built cottages and finding filth and debris, all four cottages lacked tenants. Evidence of tramp activity lay scattered about the disused yards. Number eight, Alice's old home, was devoid of its rear door leading into the scullery. The stench had knocked him sick, so he had not attempted to enter.

Once more he looked up the darkening street and decided that he would not see Alice's sister Cissy tonight. Despondently he returned to his lodgings.

Every day for a week he had stood by the small alley watching. Fresh faces came and went from the occupied buildings on the short street, but Cissy did not show herself. When a police officer challenged him, he mumbled an excuse and left, determined to return.

The pottery informed him that Joe Allerton had left their employment years ago. They were sorry but they did not know where he had gone. Hour after hour, he sat in the park throwing breadcrumbs to the hungry birds, which on spotting a meal milled around his feet in gangs. He had kicked out at the larger pigeons to prevent them from messing on the soft leather of his boots.

He had swapped his greasy flat cap for a wide-brimmed Stetson, which now lay on his lap as he fingered it gently. A young woman approached him and apprehensively said.

'Excuse me, but I must speak to you.' The bonny round face blushed slightly, and a nervous smile twitched her mouth. She had her pale gold hair tied back severely with a fashionable hat pinned on her head at a flattering angle. Her clothes were smart but practical. The full skirt and tight-boned bodice were a dark plum-coloured gabardine, which matched her hat perfectly. An ebony, black-fringed shawl hung over her shoulders against the early evening breeze.

On her approach, he had stood and slightly bowed his head in acknowledgement. He towered above her as he indicated for her to sit on the bench he had vacated. They sat on opposite ends of the bench and after an awkward moment of silence, she spoke again.

'I've seen you watching the house, but I was unsure of how to approach you.' She swallowed before continuing. 'I hope I am correct in thinking that you are a person whom I knew as Geordie?' For a fleeting moment she saw his expression change from a pleasant surprise to one of disgust, but he smiled reassuringly and nodded. 'I'm sorry. Does that offend you?' She apologised. He shook his head and with a deep voice answered.

'My name is Charles Bingham, but I used to be known as Geordie a long time ago.' His voice still held the Tyneside lilts, but the vowels were much softer.

'You may not remember me.' She lifted her face and looked directly into his eyes.

'Well, I know that you are not Alice, the hair is the wrong colour. But you do have the bonny features and a cheeky smile of a certain Cissy Allerton.' The smile on Cissy's face grew wider and more confident. She hung her head demurely as he said. 'By you have grown up into a real lady, if I may say so?' He nodded approvingly at her appearance. 'You have done well Cissy.'

'Thank you very much; I can't take all the credit; my guardian Mrs Harvey has helped to groom me. I know that I should not pry but why have you stood in the cut day after day? People would stand there just after... well you know. It was awful when they stared at the house and tried to see in the window. Alice used to shout at them to go away.' He sighed heavily.

'I'm sorry. I was trying to catch sight of you to ask what had happened to you all. You see your Guardian terrifies me.'

'She is not up to frightening anyone these days.' Her sadness was obvious to him.

'Oh, has she gone then? I never thought of that.' He looked apologetic.

'No, nothing like that but she has had a stroke and is bedridden.' She told him of how her life had changed since her mother had died. About Joe's marriage and Alice and Flo living in the country close by Ayton, where Eddie and George worked on a farm. He listened patiently, somehow, she was incredibly sad and hurting inside. Her eyes did not have the sparkle of happiness although her voice lifted excitedly as she told her tale.

He wondered perhaps that she regretted having to care for Mrs Harvey when she should be enjoying her youth. Ageing parents often called upon their daughters to care for them, but Mrs Harvey was only a neighbour. He did not press the issue and

Cissy omitted Mathew from her story.

'Do you think that Alice might see me?' He asked her nervously fingering his hat.

'I'm not sure. I could write to her if you wish.' She liked this new 'Geordie'. She had not really had much to do with the old 'Geordie', but Charles Bingham as he now called himself was a gentleman.

'No. No, I would prefer to surprise her. We did not part on good terms. I need to explain things to her. Ayton is not too far; I could easily take a ride out there.' This was the news for which he was hoping. Alice was nearby and Cissy did not mention marriage or even an engagement. He hoped and prayed that she would welcome him and listen to what he had to say.

'Well, I'm sure she would hear you out. Our Alice has always been fair.'

'That's settled then. I will go in a couple of days. I have some business to settle here first.' There was a new spring in his step as he bowed farewell to the delightful young lady.

THIRTEEN

'Come back here Flo.' Alice shouted at the back of her daughter's head. Her face was taught with anger. She had been difficult lately. Alice blamed herself, she thought she would settle after taking her away from Mrs Samuelson, but Flo was still punishing her for the withdrawal of the affection and attention she had always received from her previous employer.

'It's no good shouting behind her back Alice. You should know that.' Mrs Ford was up to her elbows in flour.

'She can be so infuriating at times Cook.' Alice went back to the pastry. 'I'm sure she does this on purpose, and she's getting worse.'

'Ah, she's fine Hinny, don't worry, she did the dishes before she left.' Cook was not a good liar and concentrated on the bread dough so as not to give the game away. The child had not done a stroke of real work for weeks.

'She gets away with far too much. If the master ever found out, she would be out on her ear. I said right at the start that she wouldn't be a particularly good kitchen maid.'

'Aye but I know that, but if she couldn't stay neither would you, look at the lovely light touch you have with pastry.' This was the truth. Alice had learnt well at her time at the Bakery. 'Master David knows how she is, look at the books he has given her to do her sketching and writing. She's a good girl at heart and clever an all.' Flour billowed into the air as Cook wiped her hands on her apron.

'I've always known she was smarter than she looks. Mrs Samuelson was teaching her how to read lips and sign her name when she was only four. She misses that and I can't spend enough time with her.'

'You're her sister pet, not her keeper.' Their real relationship had remained a well-guarded secret. In a way, it was true as they still shared the same shameful father. The Samuelson's knew how things were between Flo and Alice, but then her life with them had been more secure, or so she thought. She had learnt a great deal from Mr and Mrs Samuelson about life and how to deal with Flo's disability. Getting away from the grime and depression of the slum she had once called home had been the best thing she could have done. Her limbs had grown strong, and her hair and eyes shone with new vitality.

'She learns from the people she sees. You worry too much.' She hated to see Alice torture herself over the wayward girl.

'Aye perhaps you're right but I'm sure she's ...well, not well.'

'What do you mean?' The cook declared. 'She's the picture of health.'

'I know, but...' Alice had noted that of late Flo looked peaky and was not eating her meals.

'Look, lass!' Cook interrupted. 'You've been here over seven years and she's what? Fourteen? She is growing up that's all. She is a fine bonny lass. Rounded in all the right places, strong and healthy. I was the eldest of ten and watched them all grow. Take it from me she needs to stretch her legs and find her place. She'll settle soon enough'.

'I know all that Cook but she's been acting strangely for weeks. I just can't put my finger on it, but there is something wrong.'

When Alice first arrived at Ayton Hall, she was terrified

that she and Flo would not fit in, but all the staff had been kind. In two weeks, she would be thirty years old, but she was feeling far from old. Life was full, she always went to bed tired but not as exhausted as she used to be. Her workmates were also her friends and now the boys called to see her every week, yes life was incredibly good. Or it would be if she could only decide what was wrong with Flo and how she could deal with her wayward ways. Could there be something of Nell in her, or was it simply that she should have left her with Mrs Samuelson?

The offer from the widowed baker to take Flo as her own did not come as a surprise, the woman doted on the child. And Flo adored Mrs Samuelson. She would follow behind the older woman everywhere she went. They spent hours together as Flo learnt to write and lip read. Alice still had the book giving instructions of sign language in her bedroom. Flo and Mrs Samuelson looked through it together every day. Since the day they left to move back north Flo had not picked the book up. Alice felt she could never replace her beloved teacher.

* * *

Oblivious to her mother's call Flo hurried out of the kitchen and through the yard. Her sketchpad and pencils were tucked into a huge cloth bag, which her mother had helped her to make. It was a pretty fabric that had once been an embroidered cape. Alice had skilfully cut away the worn lining and kept the intricate quilted fabric of her mother's favourite garment. Two large squares of cloth had formed a special bag for Flo's books. She was thrilled with the result and carried it everywhere just as Nell had once worn the cape wherever she went.

A light breeze had risen to dispel the mugginess of the hot July day. Rain clouds had already begun to gather over the nearby hills with the promise of a storm. She had felt restless and heady for days. The urge to abandon the dark scullery and its endless pile of dirty dishes were too great. Today she needed to feel the sun on her face and breathe the fresh air.

Her back was aching, and her legs felt heavy. She likened herself to the carriage horses, dull and dowdy until they were set free to run in the fields when they would kick up their huge legs and run wild, mane and tail streaming behind. As she ran her spirits lifted, and she began to feel better. She slowed her pace as she neared the old barn. They never arranged a time to meet but would each arrive at the hayloft whenever they could. She might sit all day and he may not show.

At the top of the barn, the loft window opened out to the breath-taking view of the distant rolling hills, beyond which lay the desolate moorland. The house lay out of sight on the other side of a small wood. On a cloudless day, it was possible to see the buildings of Ayton Beck Farm where bother Eddie lived and worked with his wife and baby, and George, of course.

The beck meandered its way from a point up in the hills, down between her hayloft and the distant farm. Small groves of trees and bushes lay alongside the steep banks of the small river. Natural shallow pools had developed over time, which made excellent watering places for farm animals, foxes and the occasional child wishing to paddle her feet in the cool water.

It may have been the threat of a storm leaving the air heavy which made her feel unwell, but by the time Flo had reached the barn, she felt quite poorly. Her head had begun to throb unmercifully, and she felt sick. In the cool shady loft, she lay on the dry sweet-smelling hay gratefully, closed her eyes and slept.

She woke with a start. Pain gripped her stomach and back forcing her onto her knees. Crouching on all fours like an animal she held her breath until the pain subsided. With relief, she sat back against a pile of hay, beads of perspiration collecting on her forehead. Her skin was hot, and her face flushed. She inhaled deeply until her head felt light and giddy. She took a drink from the flask of water that she had fortunately filled before leaving the house. After being out in the sun with no refreshment, this had become a habit.

She sipped slowly at the liquid and then relaxed back into the hay. Moments later the pain hit her again. This time it lasted longer and was much stronger. Confused and frightened Flo lay on the hay with her knees up she rolled from side to side in agony. Once more the pain subsided, and she lay exhausted until the pain returned. She felt a rush of warm liquid flow down her thighs. Quickly she pulled at her skirts and removed the wet draws. The blood-stained wet underwear frightened her. Whatever was happening to her she did not know. She was in pain, alone and very scared.

The next pain took her breath, and she pushed against the pain inside her. She sat against the mound of hay, her arms supporting her back, her knees bent and parted. As an excruciating wave of pain hit her, she forced her whole body down with a huge effort. Blood spurted from between her legs and spread slowly among the strands of prickly straw.

Lying between her thighs was a small perfectly formed baby. Flo stared down at the lifeless infant. She sat with her arms across her knees, her hot forehead resting on her arms and tears mingling with the sweat on her face. When more pain hit her, she leant to one side and vomited.

* * *

Casually he whistled tunelessly as he approached the barn. The sun was still hot, and he would be relieved to sit in the shade for a while. When he didn't see Flo waiting at the entrance, he was a little perturbed, he needed her today. He had had a particularly difficult, day the softness of her body would help him relax but after that fight, she had been frightened off. He loved to see her drawings but when he saw the sketch of him in the nude, he was angry and had torn it from the book.

As he neared the ladder to the hayloft, he could smell something strange. Not the usual country smell of cattle, pigs and newly mown grass, this was a sickly stench. He climbed the ladder with caution. When his head appeared followed by his shoulders Flo saw the movement and sat watching him. His face held a look of pure horror at the sight before him. Blood covered the straw-strewn floor as if a pig had been freshly slaughtered. By Flo's feet lay a small baby still attached to the umbilical cord. The tiny form, purple to blue, was not much bigger than his hand. The afterbirth dark red, like a whole liver lay partially covered with straw as if an animal had tried to store it away lay nearby.

Flo had the sketchpad and pencil poised; the page was covered in drawings of the child in front of her.

He stood frozen; his mouth agape unable to utter a sound. Suddenly gaining his senses he leapt forward into the loft grabbing Flo by the shoulders he pulled her to her feet.

'You stupid little bitch.' He shook her violently. 'Get rid of it and don't you dare tell anyone; do you understand?' She looked blankly back at him. He pushed her away from him with a force fuelled by disgust and she staggered to keep her balance before falling hard against the loft wall. Menacingly he bent over her prostrate body. She was sobbing with fear, holding her arm over her face to protect it from his wrath she did not see his words. 'You name me, and I'll deny ever laying a finger on you.' As he left the loft, he kicked loose straw over the baby's corpse, he left Flo rocking herself in grief and stealthily he made for the hills.

Eventually, Flo wrapped the dead infant lovingly in her petticoat and held it to her for five minutes. The small face peeped out from under the folds of the white cotton; gently she kissed its cold cheek then put the bundle into her cloth bag.

❋ ❋ ❋

Well hidden by trees and bushes growing close to the river edge the travel-worn figure washed his aching feet. His clothes were nothing more than dirty rags fastened together with string. Everyone turned him away from every house he begged at due to the smell that hung around his unwashed body. The little hair he had left on his head hung long and greasy. He lost his teeth either in a brawl or rotted away. Life on the road had not been his intention; he much preferred a warm bed and a daily meal, but those days were well and truly over. For months now he had walked the roads looking for handouts. With all his money gone, crippled with pain and his family lost to him he could only eke out an existence begging or stealing.

While his feet soaked in the cool water, he tore more strips of fabric from his threadbare coat to line his worn boots. He hoped the big house beyond the woods, would prove fruitful. A cleaner appearance might help. As he tried in vain to clean the dirt and smell from his body, a movement further upstream caught his eye. He sat back further into the cover of the foliage he saw a young girl. She wadded into the middle of the fast-flowing stream until the water was playing just above her bare knees. With her skirts held up over her young round figure, she began to wash her legs. The tramp could not help but react to her movements, as her hands caressed her thighs. Her hands moved up and down and her body bent and swayed with the action. He licked his lips and shuddered involuntarily.

It was a long time since he had felt the warmth of a woman. Hurriedly he replaced his boots never letting the girl out of his sight. After she had washed the girl stood momentarily in the flow of the water looking downstream. Around her body hung a large heavily weighted cloth bag. He watched her remove it and hold it up to her face. She was kissing the cloth or was she just looking deep into it? The foliage which he used to hide his presence also obscured his view. Making it difficult to see exactly what she was up to, but she was certainly acting very strangely.

The tramp pulled back in surprise as she hurled the bag into the centre of the stream and then wadded gingerly back to the bank. The bundle sailed slowly downstream towards the hidden tramp as he watched it with fascination. He glanced back to where he had last seen the girl, but all he saw was bare the riverbank. She had gone.

The bundle had snagged on a branch just three feet from where he stood. His curiosity aroused he looked about for a way to retrieve the bundle. He had to see what was in it. Using a long spidery branch torn from a nearby bush he released the cloth bag and teased the bundle towards him until it lay by his feet on the side of the riverbank.

Curiously, he peered into the bag. He carefully removed the bundle of cotton and straw and began to unwrap it. A small hand fell from the folds of cotton, and he dropped the bundle in horror. He shuddered in disgust and with his boot, he kicked the tiny corpse back into the stream. Turning his attention back to the cloth bag he was about to kick that back into the water also when a distant memory struck him.

Forgotten images of long ago, of a young woman in a cape, then a dark, damp kitchen and children crying. He could hear the stupid babblings of a crazy woman who had stolen his savings.

'Alice!' He spat as the name hit his lips and stuffed the remains of his wife's quilted cape into his pocket and set out to find the girl from the river.

FOURTEEN

C harles rode the chestnut brown stallion with ease. He had found horse riding difficult at first, but necessary to navigate the cattle ranges of America. An old, experienced rancher had jokingly brought him a carthorse to ride.

'Git yer great lanky legs around that.' The old man had laughed, but the animal was calm and sedate and taught Charles quickly. He was soon quite at home on any horse. He may not have been a 'natural' rider, but a confident one.

He walked his hired horse through the tall imposing gates of High Fell House. No one challenged his entry, so he continued along the wide, gravelled winding driveway. The place appeared deserted. He took the path that he believed would lead to the rear of the house and the servant's entrance. The expected bustle of the stable yard was absent. A horse whinnied at his approach and a dog barked but no one greeted him. He dismounted his horse and tied him close to a feed trough. Puddles of rainwater lay over the rough, gravelled yard after the previous night's thunderstorms, so avoiding the scattered puddles that lay over the yard he walked towards the back of the house.

A shout rang out across the yard.

'Oi, you there. Can I help yer?' Charles turned to see a small middle-aged man hobbling slowly on bent rickety legs in his direction. The various strips of leather and brasses that hung over his shoulders weighed him down still further.

'I was looking for Alice Allerton, I was told she was the assistant cook here.' The small man grimaced in what one may have mistaken for a smile.

'Aye. She does, but it is not a good day to come visiting. Her sister Flo didn't come home last night and the 'ole house is out looking for her.'

'I really need to see Miss Allerton. I've travelled a long way.' The old stable hand rubbed his large bulbous nose and looked thoughtful.

'I'll go an' see what cook say's.' He waddled off in the general direction of the kitchen, the brass buckles swung pendulously over his back knocking at his buttocks and tapping out his steps.

Charles stood in the doorway of the large warm kitchen that smelt of new bread and cinnamon. He held his large hat by the rim and nervously spun it around in his hands. Mrs Ford's large 'comfortable' frame squeezed into an old oak carver chair. The solid wooden arms dug into her sides giving the impression that her body moulded into the seat. A mug of steaming liquid rested in her soft pudding hands. Her voice had a slow comforting sound.

'Come in an' sit down if yer would. Me necks aching looking up at yer.' He obliged and sat on a low bench on the other side of the black leaded range. 'Now young man, you were asking about Alice.' Charles nodded. 'She's never told us anything about a big strapping lad like you. except Eddie her brother, who works over on yon farm, but you could make two of him and no problems or doubts about it.'

'I left a long time ago. I used to be a friend of the family way back.' He did not wish to enlighten the woman too much of his history.

'Has Ged told you about the lass being missing?' She leant forward as if sharing a conspiracy.

'Only that she didn't come home.'

'Aye, well, Alice is out of her mind with worry. Do you know that the lass is a deaf-mute?' Charles nodded. 'Lovely with it though. We all think the world of them both. She can be a handful, young Flo that is, but she's never been out all night.' Mrs Ford sipped at the steaming tea, nodding towards a door to her left she continued. 'I hope she's asleep, never got a wink all night, she hasn't. I have never seen two sisters so close, likely because of her disability I expect.' Charles sat quietly and allowed the matronly woman to chatter on.

'Mr Evans is sitting with her; he thinks the world of her. 'Course he doesn't think I've noticed, but he is smitten. He'll do anything for her.' Panic rose in Charles's mind; he had never thought that Alice might have become involved with someone else. The cook continued to sip her tea. Charles sat quietly watching her face, her whole demeanour added to the warmth of the kitchen and the cosy smells had such a calming effect on him. For five minutes the only sound was that of the huge mantle clock ticking rhythmically.

'Cook. Cook.' Both Mrs Ford and Charles jumped to their feet in surprise, although the rounded woman took a little longer to reach her standing position. A young boy flung himself through the door, breathless with running and his eyes alight with excitement.

'Have they found her?' The cook was hopeful.

'No, but Alfie and Master David have found her drawing book.' Mrs Ford had her hand over her mouth hardly daring to breathe. A group of men stood in the open doorway; Charles stood aside to allow them to enter. A smartly dressed youth hugged Mrs Ford reassuringly.

'Don't worry Cook. This might be good news; we don't know for sure.' He spoke well, without a northern accent, obviously very well educated. 'This must be the young master.' Charles thought.

'What do you mean Mr David?' The youth took her back to the oak carver chair.

'We've found her sketchbook up in the old barn over on

the top field.' He took a deep breath. 'The floor was strewn with blood-stained straw.' The cook gasped in horror. 'The men have started searching along the river and up to the moors behind. Don't upset yourself Cook it's not her blood. I'm sure.' Charles was sure that this young fellow knew more. He was hiding something, there was more to this and Mr David, Charles stepped forward.

'May I introduce myself?' David looked up at the stranger whom he had not noticed when he first entered.

'Please do.' He replied politely.

'Charles Bingham, I'm an old friend of Alice's. I have been out of the country and have travelled a long way to see Alice only to find all this commotion. I want to help if I can?' The two men shook hands. David nodded.

'I'm pleased to meet you, Mr Bingham. I am David Fleetham, and this is my father's house who, fortunately, is away at present and unaware of the commotion as you call it. He would not be pleased to know that his whole household is out looking for a missing kitchen maid.' David glanced around the kitchen as he spoke. 'Have you seen Alice yet?' He asked the newcomer.

'No. Cook here told me that she is asleep.'

'No, I'm not.' Alice entered the kitchen. She saw the sketchpad in David's hand, rushed forward and snatched it from him, her whole attention on the battered book she did not notice the tall visitor. She hugged the book to her chest and then looked up to plead for information.

Her mouth fell open, and she staggered slightly as she saw the face which had haunted her over the years, the face that had crept into her dreams and nightmares. That face had been there at every tragic turn in her life, and it was here again. Like a bad penny, he was there. She was not really surprised to see him even after all these years.

He was the spectre of bad tidings. Her Jonah. When he stepped forward and spoke her name, she realised that he was real and not in her wild imagination. David and Mr Evans led her to a chair. 'The Butler.' Thought Charles. 'He's much too old for her.'

Alice stared up at the face from the past. She could not speak. Her head shook ever so slightly in denial that he was there in front of her. Charles crossed to where Alice sat dumfounded and knelt in front of her. She was too shocked to respond to his touch when he took her hand. She wanted to pull away but found herself frozen in time.

The straight-backed, upright Mr Evans watched her reactions carefully. He scrutinised her face for any emotion. He wanted to know who this tall handsome man was and what his connection might be with Alice. He liked order and precision. This stranger was not supposed to be here. He could feel the tension between Alice and Charles.

'Alice.' Charles waited for her reply, but she did not speak. The surrounding air seemed to tingle with electricity and Owen Evans was confused. Charles spoke again. 'Alice, I'm sorry. I didn't mean for us to meet again in such circumstances.' She could not look at him anymore. The air was stifling. As the tears began to well in her eyes, she pushed him away and ran from the kitchen into the yard and on into the well-stocked and cultivated vegetable garden.

Charles found her sitting on the low surrounding wall bent double and crying incessantly. He sat down beside her. It hurt him to see her small sobbing form so delicate and vulnerable next to his huge frame.

'I'm sorry that this has been such a shock for you Alice. Believe me, it is not the way I had imagined our reunion. Please, Alice.' He pleaded.

Through the sobs, she nodded and managed a brief smile.

'Yes.' Her body quivered with a huge sigh as she tried to speak through her grief.

'I've seen Cissy, and she told me everything. I'll not spoil anything for you here, I promise.' She nodded her head. 'When I left you, I found myself in America of all places. I wanted to build a new life and prove to you that I could change. Well, it took me a bit longer than I thought it would, but I am back now. Look at me Alice, I'm made up.' He opened his arms in a wide gesture to show how he had changed.

She saw a big handsome man. The sun had tanned his face and fine lines around his eyes from squinting gave him a happy smiling face. His thick, black hair was a bit on the long side to be tidy, but he was well-groomed. The smell of new leather and shaving soap emanated from him. A smile played on her lips as she remembered the huge, grubby dockworker who had almost proposed marriage.

'Right now, Geordie I am only worried about Flo. You always do have a way of turning up when there was trouble, or even starting it'

'Even me Ma used to say that. 'Charlie' She called me. 'Yer nowt but bloody trouble'. Then if she couldn't reach to belt me, she would throw whatever came to hand. She threw a flat iron once, it would have taken my head off if I hadn't ducked, instead, it made a great big hole in the wall before it hit the ground and bounced on my sister Mary's foot. 'Course I'd scarpered before Mary got a chance to finish the job with her fist. Big girl our Mary.'

'They won't find her.' Alice had not heard him. 'She's been out all night in that storm. It's not like her.' She began to look through the sketchpad that up until now she had been hugging tightly to herself like a child with a favourite toy. 'Look.' She held the first page up to Charles. 'She's good, isn't she? She drew that picture of me a few weeks ago. And these...' Alice turned to a page full of cruel caricatures of the household. 'If Owen saw that he'd burst his braces.' Charles watched her slowly turn the pages. 'The child has talent.' He thought.

The butler's voice called out to Alice. Quickly she slammed the book closed, afraid that Owen Evens the straitlaced butler would see the offending cartoons. The small party made their way back to the house, Charles walking a little way behind. He was trying to weigh up the stiff butler, the same way that he himself had been by the butler.

FIFTEEN

Tired hurt and angry Flo had walked for miles. Her stomach ached, and blood still dripped from her. Her hands were scratched and dirty from grasping the foliage to aid her weary body up the steep hillside. The rain came with a clap of thunder, which she did not hear, and a flash of light, which she did see. Her wet clothes clung to her body and legs hindering her progress even more.

The surrounding scenery grew sparser as she entered the rough moors. Dark shadows scampered away as she disturbed flocks of sheep. Eventually, completely exhausted, she sat among the prickly gorse bushes and wept.

He found her curled up like a small child, sound asleep. The dawn had broken shrouded in mist after the downpour. He did not wake her, instead, he lit a small fire close by and sat watching her sleep. The rabbit that he had snared the previous evening roasted over the fire and he boiled a small pan of water over the embers. He had enough tea leaves to make a weak mug of tea but no milk or sugar to sweeten it. Flo stirred, and with a groan, she gripped her stomach as she rose.

'Good, yer awake then.' Completely unaware that she was unable to hear his gruff voice. Dazed and confused she sat staring at the dirty and very smelly tramp. He handed her the remains of his tea, but she did not take it from him. 'Please yersel,' He growled as he swigged back the remaining drops of grey liquid. 'Hungry?' She read his lips and shook her head. The thought of taking food from his filthy hands almost caused her to vomit. 'It's the first bit of meat I've 'ad in days so it'll not go to waste.'

He didn't look or speak to her again until the whole rabbit had been gone, leaving bones and skin, then he wiped his greasy hands over his grimy trousers and the sleeve of his jacket functioned as a napkin for the grease on his mouth and face. As he prodded the dying embers of the fire, he spoke again.

'Well, I guess you wouldn't want to talk to me. Few people do. But, well I got to thinking while you were asleep. 'Cos you 'ad Nell's cape, well what's left of it anyway. I reckoned you must know me daughter Alice.' He looked at her frightened face. 'You do know Alice, don't you?'

Flo had read the words 'NO ALICE.' He did not form his words well enough for her to read all that he said. She captured the odd word but not enough to make sense.

'If I were to guess RIGHT, you'd BE the BRAT she 'ad, an yer SEE that WOOD make me yer Da. So, as YOU is about...' He tried to count the years on his fingers but failed. 'WELL, yer underage, SEW by my reckoning I'd be yer legal guardian.' Flo frowned as she tried to make sense of the few words she had caught. 'Don't LUCK so scared.' He leaned towards her menacingly and she shied away from the stench emanating from his mouth. 'You 'n ME is GOING to get along GRATE.' When he grinned, his few stumpy blackened teeth stuck out in weird angles from his mouth. She had never seen anything so disgusting before and she grimaced in horror.

'Don't you be laughing at me girl?' He bellowed. 'I'm yer bleeding guardian angel 'n you are gonna learn to respect that. You might not be much to look at now but when I get yer cleaned up yer could earn me a bob or two. Aye, I know a few who'd pay well for a few of your favours.' Flo had closed her eyes against his ugliness keeping her ignorant of his plans for her future.

He struggled to his feet, cursing his cramped limbs. Flo

tried to pull away from him as he reached out and grabbed her arms but small as he was and in her weakened state, she was no match for his strength. Her resistance met with a heavy slap across her face, leaving her skin glowing red and stinging. He tied his long thin coat belt tightly around her right wrist while she was still dazed by the blow. He left the hot embers of the fire to burn itself out and dragged Flo across the moor.

With his poor daughter in tow, he set off to walk to Stokesley, where he knew he would find customers willing to pay for her services. He kept well to the side of the road and whenever he heard an approaching cart or rider, he pushed the hapless girl into the bushes which lined the way. Her lack of protest he took as a willingness to comply. In truth, she was mourning the loss of her child and the desertion of her lover.

She did not have the strength or will to fight so she quietly staggered where Bert led. If she had caught enough of his words to understand her fate, then she may have found the energy to struggle.

❊ ❊ ❊

The earlier storm left the morning fresh and sharp. The grass glistened in the early morning light. George wandered across the sloping fields down towards the swollen stream. His constant companions, Bess, and Ed the sheepdogs were by his side and were proving to be excellent workers. Bess was beginning to understand the complicated whistles. He let out a long piercing tone, which should have brought the young dog to heel but she was otherwise engaged in the bushes.

'Now what do you think Ed?' He questioned the pup, named after his brother due to the striking resembles of the long gangly legs. 'Do you think she heard us and is just feeling independent, or do you think she is just deaf or stupid?' The dog yapped a short reply. 'Aye, she is just a little stupid. I expect she is after us fetching her.' The Shepard blew air in an exasperated sigh as he began to walk towards the errant pup. As he neared the bushes, the young Collie appeared from the undergrowth and barked at its master. Before George could catch the animal, it had dived back into the thicket. 'Stupid animal.' He muttered as he fell to his knees.

Crawling on all fours he followed the dog under the bush. 'Blasted dog.' He cursed. 'What have you found that is so bloody exciting?' The dog barked and leapt about around a bundle of rags. George lay right out on his belly and stretched his arms out to reach the dog's find. He gently pulled the wet bundle towards him, hampered by the pup bouncing and yapping around him knocking the wet dew from the branches above him and soaking the back of George's neck. With a loud grunt, he grasped the cloth and pulled it into the open.

The dog lay down with his nose as close to the find as it knew his master would allow. Sitting back on his haunches George began to unwrap the tattered cloth. He looked down on the bloated face of a new-born infant.

'Oh, God!' He exclaimed quietly like a prayer. The dog seemed pleased with his find and began to yap once more to his master as if asking for praise. When none was forthcoming, he moved silently to Georges side and waited for further instructions? The young Shepherds mind was in turmoil, he could not leave the poor mite here. He removed his jacket and very carefully wrapped the dead infant up.

With the dogs walking quietly beside him as if in tune with his mood George carried his wretched find to the farm, blissfully unaware that he was taking his niece's baby daughter to her final resting place.

'Best take it to Stokesley or Northallerton for the authorities to sort out.' Said Mr Cooper matter of factually. 'Found many a dead animal in that yon beck after a storm but never a poor baby.' His wife Elsie shed a tear for the poor dead infant as she laid it gently in the small wooden crate lined with straw. It was too much for her to bear seeing the tiny corpse in the makeshift coffin.

'Take it away George. Please.' She turned away from the sight that brought back too many memories of her own lost babies.

The small rough coffin lay on the back of the flat cart guarded by the two black and white Collie dogs as George took the sad journey. Ayton was too small to house a police station, so he decided to go on to Stokesley.

The road was rough going; the uneven road bounced and slew the light cart through every pothole and rut. The load was usually heavy enough to steady the cart; today was the exception with its sad cargo.

George's heart was heavy, not only with the errand but also with the news from Middlesbrough. Cissy had written to the Coopers to inform them that Tess Harvey was ill and not expected to live. It was years now since her first stroke, which had left her bedridden and dependent on Cissy. Two more strokes had weakened her further and had affected her heart the doctor had said. He remembered the old neighbour. She had been the one who had parcelled the two unfortunate little boys off to stay with her sister Elsie in the country, and for this Eddie and he would always be grateful.

He saw the tramp in the distance, it frightened him to think that without the generosity of the Mr and Mrs Cooper he and his brother might have ended up on the road. The tramp's grey coat swung with each step, while the tin cans and bottles that hung from his waist bounced and danced around him clattering out a rhythm. As he neared, he realised that the tramp was not alone. He had something or someone on a leash. It was difficult to make out what, it walked well to the side of the road almost obscured by the bushes, which lined the way.

When the tramp heard the oncoming cart, he turned and glared menacingly at the driver. George took the look as a warning and gave the scruffy individual a wide berth. There was something about the dirty unshaven face that made him uneasy. The young dog in the back of the cart barked protectively, and the tramp appeared to growl back at the animal. George was certain that he had seen the man before. He shrugged his shoulders in bewilderment. 'Must have just seen him about the area.' He thought.

He paid little attention to the person on the other end of the leash, his quick glance back at the duo showed that it was a girl or young boy but no more.

'Quiet Bess.' His dog ceased barking, and he continued his way.

❊   ❊   ❊

Darkness had fallen by the time George returned to the farm. The police had asked questions about his finding of the infant. Where did he find it? Did he see who left it? Did he know the mother? How long ago was it born? He was beginning to wish he had left the poor mite in the river in peace. They were only doing their job, but he was a bit put out that they thought he had had a hand in the infant's demise. Eventually, he could leave when he had drawn his cross on a statement of the facts, as he knew them. It was times like this that he wished he had learned all his letters when he and Eddie were at Sunday school.

Elsie Cooper had his supper ready for him.

'Eddie has gone over to see Alice.' She told him. 'Something about young Flo being missing. Alice is in a right state.'

'Flo is often away for hours at a time why the panic?' He replied between mouthfuls of hot lamb broth. Mr Cooper sat by the fire sucking on his favourite pipe. There was no tobacco in the bowl.

Mrs Cooper hated him smoking in the kitchen.

'Seems she didn't come home at all last night. Stayed out in the storm. My guess is she's run off with that lad.' He tapped the empty pipe against the arm of the chair and gained a scolding from his wife in the form of a scathing look that could fell an ox.

'What lad?' George spoke with his mouth full of food, rushing it down in order that he could join his brother and find out what was really happening over at the big house.

'I've seen her up on the hills with a lad a few times. There's nowt wrong with my eyes even if my legs are a bit stiff.' He would always talk about how he was getting too old for farming. Elsie would not agree with this as the last thing she wanted was him hanging around the house all day, even if she did love the big lump. 'Yer can tell her off for miles cos she's always waving 'er arms about, but I don't know who the lad was. Tallish and I think he had dark hair. Couldn't be sure though he usually wore a cap.'

'Did you tell Eddie this?'

'Nope. Didn't think anything of it till I'd had a chance to think about it.' He winked across at his wife. 'I can always think better with me pipe.'

'What makes you think that she's run off with this lad?' The fork clattered to the plate as George finished his meal.

'It's not my place to criticise how the lass is brought up, but I wouldn't let my Lizzie run about the hills like a wild thing even if she was a bit mental.'

'She's not mental Boss she's deaf.' He pushed his chair away from the table as he spoke scraping it noisily across the stone floor. My Cooper shrugged his shoulders.

'Same thing.'

'No, it's not. She can't hear what you say but she can understand what people say if they speak clearly, and she can read and write which is more than I can.'

'Only 'cos you couldn't be bothered to learn, and if she's not daft why does she make all those queer noises?'

'I'm sorry Bos but right now I haven't got the time to get into this. I must get to the Big House.' He was pulling on his overcoat against the evening chill as he spoke. He took his battered cap off the peg behind the door.

'I'll call into old Jack's cottage 'n ask him to call in the morning to help with the milking in case we're not back.' He dashed out leaving the old farmer chuntering to his wife about the way the youngters went on today.

SIXTEEN

Alice sat quietly on the edge of the smooth well-made, large iron bed. The clean crisp sheets and counterpane drew tight. Until six weeks ago she had shared this paradise of a room, and bed, with Flo. She thought back to how hurt she had been when Flo had asked if she could share a room with young Doris the under housemaid.

'Why would you want to move,' she had asked her, but Flo gave no reply, just shrugged her shoulders. Cook had said at the time that youngsters needed their own space.

'You must have felt that yourself when you were young Alice?' How could she have ever felt that? Caring for her siblings in one dark dingy room she had had no time to think like a normal young girl. There had been no time for thoughts of individuality, space, or time then or since. Even after leaving the slum, she had called home, she had Flo to care for. All her energies had gone into caring for her daughter. They had fought the disability together, teaching one another to communicate, it had been challenging work. But with the help of kind friends such as the Samuelson's at the bakery, they had, she thought succeeded. Flo had pushed her mother's patience and endurance to the extreme limit. She had almost lost the position here at the Hall when the master had found out Flo was deaf.

The young master David had pleaded with his father to

allow her to stay. He had seen her talent and nurtured it by giving her unlimited paper and lead pencils. Slowly Alice turned the pages of her daughter's sketchbook. She absorbed every line and shadow on the pages. Here was Flo's life. Her thoughts and feelings flowed into the charcoal and pencil images.

Alice smiled as she remembered the day Flo had sketched this picture. They were both in the kitchen with Cook who had fallen asleep by the fire. Flo had drawn Alice as she kneaded the bread dough. Every detail was captured. The strands of hair around her face had broken free from the band holding her long hair back. Even the powdery flour on her arms and nose was so realistic. Looking at the pictures helped Alice feel closer to Flo. Reading her diary could not have been any more personal.

As she turned the pages Alice's joy turned to dismay. The black and grey images danced before her eyes. Her knuckles whitened as she gripped the edges of the book to stop it from shaking.

'Oh my God!' She exclaimed softly as she desperately tried to swallow the hard lump that formed in her throat. Her thoughts and emotions ran wildly through her head. Jumping from shock, horror, pity and remorse then back again to shock and anger. Questions shouted at her. How did she come to this? The pictures were of such a graphic nature. Who? When? Where would Flo see the nakedness of this kind?

A gentle tap on the door startled her. Hurriedly she hid the book and its offending pages under her apron before Cook entered.

'Oh Hinny.' She prattled at Alice like she was a sick child. 'Did you get any sleep? No, I don't suppose you would.' She answered herself as if Alice were incapable of speaking. She had brought her a tray of tea and choice slices of her best cake. As the cook busied herself noisily with the contents of the tray she chatted on. 'There's no more news. Here, drink this pet it will help. I've laced it with a drop of honey and a tot of brandy.' Cook pressed the delicate cup into Alice's hand.

'Ahem.' The discrete cough came from the open doorway.

Alice looked up at Geordie who filled the room with his presence. Why did he always seem to be about when she was troubled? He had been there when her father had mysteriously hurt himself and became unable to work. The bad penny turned up when her two young brothers went away to slave up cold dark chimneys for a pittance. Geordie had been there when her father brutally murdered her mother. Like a spectre of doom, he feasted on trouble.

Now her daughter was missing, and he was there again. Through his years of absence, her life had seemed peaceful and without incident. Now he was back and brought misfortune on her yet again. She did not hate him or even dislike him. In fact, over the years she had often wondered what had become of her tormentor. If she had not found her mother's treasures, she may have accepted his proposal in desperation. She did not refuse him entry into the room. Cook poured him a cup of tea and then made a discrete retreat with the excuse that she had a pan of soup to deal with. For a minute, they sat in silence.

He watched her fingering the battered sketchpad.

'I've been helping with the search.' He told her. 'Believe me when I say this Alice, I am here to help in any way that I can. The weak-willed ignorant idiot who worked on the docks for beer money with the big feet and thoughtless ways has gone. I have grown up while I've been away. It took a long time I know but me Ma always said I was thick in the head as well as the skin.'

Alice listened but said nothing. She pondered on his words. He sounded different, quieter than she remembered, and his accent had altered. If only she did not have such a huge weight on her, she might be able to think straight. Her eyes closed, whilst her jaw clenched, and her lips quivered as she fought back the tears.

He stood up and slowly took the few steps to where she sat and sat gently beside her. His movements were that of a huntsman careful not to frighten the quarry. When he put his arms around her, she slumped against his body like old friends. The paired rocked slowly in unison as she sobbed out her grief and he lovingly stroked her hair. He smelt her scent, sweet lavender, and a hint of cooking herbs. Softly he spoke words of comfort as a parent might to a frightened child. Her crying eased and her breathing slowed as she fell into an exhausted sleep.

Charles cradled the woman he loved in his arms. He had loved her all those years ago but in his brash youthful immature way. If only he had stood by her when she needed him most, instead of running away at the first refusal. This time he was strong enough and mature enough to take everything she threw at him. Whatever happened, he would be there. She could batter and beat him emotionally, but he would not leave her again.

Carefully he lay her down on the bed and covered her with a soft blanket. The book fell to the floor spilling the loose pages about his feet. Once again, he marvelled at the child's talent as he reviewed the pictures.

As Alice had done, he saw the beauty and grace of the drawings of the animals and recognised the likeness of Alice. He saw again the caricatures of the household servants and many drawings of the young master David who had since introduced himself. Flo had obviously put all her heart and soul into these drawings. The loose pages held excellent pencil sketches of a naked man in various classic poses. The face of the model obliterated with black charcoal, destroying the features completely. It was doubtful that Flo herself had done it, she was an artist and would never deface her work.

At first, the drawings of the infant had not struck him as any different to the other sketches. They were beautiful and lifelike of a sleeping infant. Then his mind began to put in all together. This was her life, a sleeping infant and a naked man. Put that with the pictures of David, the carnage found with the book and her disappearance. The pieces began to fall into place. That is why the young man looked so worried about a missing kitchen maid. Young men of his high standing would not normally be heading a search for a mere serving girl. What had he done? Had he got worried when she found out she was expecting? Could he have killed them both? If he were leading the search, could he keep the men away from the bodies?

'Oh, God.' He thought. That is why Alice is so distraught, she must have also worked it out. He looked down at the sleeping woman. 'Poor Alice. My poor, poor Alice.' He bit on his fist as he pondered what he could do. He pushed the loose sheets of paper into his jacket pocket and put the book by her side then he re-joined the men in the kitchen.

❊ ❊ ❊

George strode across the yard towards the group of men breathless from his hurried journey to aid his brother who nodded at his approach. The men were discussing the progress of the search for young Flo.

'There's no sign of the lass within a ten-mile radius of here.' A farmhand aged by weather hard life spoke despairingly. 'Me 'and the lads 'ave looked everywhere.'

'Aye, 'n it's no good yer shouting for 'er is it.' The comment was not meant to be offensive but more of a fact about the girl's disability, however, the other men glowered at him, and he kicked his heavy booted foot in the dirt looking shameful for his careless words. One of his workmates took over the conversation quickly.

'Look! It'll be dark soon, so there's not much more can do tonight. Let us all get a night's rest and start again in the morning.' Bobby Baker the oldest in the group did not agree.

'Naw, the master's back the morra noon 'an 'es not gonna take very kindly to us lot wandering the hills for a bloody kitchen maid is 'e?' The tanned weather-beaten wrinkled face directed his gaze to Eddie.

'I know she's yer kin but.... well, we've done our best.'

'Aye likely she'll come home when she's good and hungry.' Said a much younger farmhand.

'You might be right there Robbie lad. And we all have beds

133

to go to and a job tomorrow what pays our keep.' The older man reasoned.

'We can keep our eyes and ears open while we go about our business.'

'Aye,' Robbie perked up with new confidence, grown from the attention of the small group. 'All the farmers' roundabouts know that the lass is missing, so they'll let on if they see owt.' The general opinion was that the search stopped, and the group dispersed leaving the two brothers staring helplessly at one another.

'Looks like it's just us two then.' George tried to sound optimistic but even he thought it was hopeless to continue. They had searched the old quarries and out beyond the moorland, every farm building and wooded area for ten miles searched thoroughly.

'I will not give up that easily, not while our Alice is so cut up. Come on let us get back to the farm. We'll start out again in the morning after milking.'

Charles watched the group from a discrete distance. The papers rustled quietly in his pocket as he fingered the torn crumpled edges and thought about the defaced drawings. He made a sudden decision and walked quickly to catch up with George and Eddie.

* * *

The light had faded completely, a dark, star-studded sky and a new moon lit up the farmyard. The three men sat around the well-scrubbed table solemnly eating a nourishing stew prepared by Elsie Cooper. The old farmer and his wife had gone to bed with a warning to Eddie not to keep his young wife and baby waiting too long. Their cottage was only ten yards down the lane from the main house, but Eddie's wife Elizabeth would not rest until her husband was 'indoors'.

Charles had relayed his life story again to the two young

134

men, and they had discussed the search party's reluctance to resume. Carefully Charles had asked Eddie what he knew about Flo and Alice's relationship. He was relieved to discover that they both knew of Flo's true parentage.

'Flo is a very talented young girl,' Charles said. The brothers nodded. George said.

'I'm regretting not learning to write and read like Flo.'

'I think Charlie boy is talking about the drawing, not the writing.' Eddie laughed at his young brother. Charles asked them if they had seen her sketchpad. They both nodded in unison.

'She does some right funny ones,' Eddie said.

'I like the horse she showed me.' Said, George. Charles took a risk and took the crumpled paper from his coat pocket.

'What do you think of these?' He smoothed out the paper and pushed them slowly towards the shocked faces.

'Bloody 'Ell.' Gasped George. Eddie was too shocked to utter anything. With a lowered voice Charles told his companions about the sketches in the book Alice now had hidden away. He then outlined his thoughts as to what might have happened. George gulped audibly and nearly choked at the thought. He spluttered out about his gruesome find.

The worry and consequent search for Flo had put all thoughts of the infant and the trip to Stokesley out of his mind until now.

'Slow down George, you're babbling.' His brother always took charge. George took a deep breath, sighed heavily, and started again.

'This morning when I was out with the dogs, we found a bundle in the river. I had to take it to Stokesley that's why I didn't know about Flo till I got back.' He closed his eyes and shook his head, taking another deep breath before continuing. 'It was a new-born baby the police officer said. This doctor fella who they called in, he said it was small and not full term, whatever that meant. I had to make a sworn statement that I 'ad just found it and not responsible for it.'

'Why didn't you tell me?' Eddie asked him a little irate that he'd had to drag the news from him.

'You weren't here. You were out on the top field. By the time I got back from town you were up there with Alice.' Charles calmed the tone down.

'Shhh... you'll wake the household shouting at one another, and it won't help.' There was silence for a moment as the three men took in the meaning of George's find.

'Right.' Charles declared. 'Let us put all this together. We know that Flo drew everything, Alice says that was her way.' Eddie nodded.

'She drew everyone comically but those people or things she loved she appeared to draw lifelike,' Eddie said. Charles continued.

'I saw pictures of Alice, young master David, this faceless man and a baby.' George's mouth was agape, and his face was red with embarrassment. Eddie did not flinch at the realisation, marriage and fatherhood had opened his mind to such things.

'If you're thinking the same as me, Charlie, we have to have words with this David.' It was hard to believe that this suggestion could have any foundation. He did not know Master David very well, but he thought it highly unlikely that he could or would hurt their Flo.

'That's what I think as well, Eddie, but we have no tangible evidence.'

George was speechless by the whole thing. His eyes went back and forth from one face to the other as they spoke. The whole thing seemed incredible.

'He was very keen to help with the search for Flo,' Eddie said.

'Was that so that he could lead us away?' Charles raised his eyebrows as he spoke.

'But he was the first to find the barn.'

'Aye! But how did he know to look there?'

'Why would he show us the barn if he knew the state it

was in?'

'His way of leading us off the scent.'

'This is all too devious for me. I cannot see why the lad would take us to that barn. There was blood everywhere, and her book lay there for all to see. You were not there Charlie. He was as shocked as anyone.'

Eddie did not believe that Master David could be responsible.

'The boss said he'd seen her with a lad.' George's voice was quiet, but Charles and Eddie turned their heads swiftly to face him. 'Mr Cooper said that he had seen Flo running the fields with a lad, but he didn't know who.'

'When did he tell you this?' Eddie questioned him.

'This afternoon when I got back from town, and he said you were all out looking for her. I nearly got into an argument with him about her.'

'Yer a mine of information our George. Why do you keep it to yourself?' His brother scolded him.

'Cos since yer got wed yer don't what to listen to me anymore.'

'Shush...Keep your voices down. You're both acting like children.' Charles had to quieten them again. 'I always remembered you too being quiet lads. Is this your way of making up for lost time? There's nothing more to say or do tonight so I suggest we all sleep and deal with it in the morning.'

Charles spent a restless night in the loft above the milking room. He was warm and comfortable; George had insisted he take the good mattress while he slept on the old straw bed, which had been his during his first years on Cooper's farm. The events of the day kept him awake. The pieces of the puzzle swam unceasingly around in his thoughts. Whom was Flo seeing? Where would she run? Did she go with the boy who got her into this trouble, or has he done her harm? Was it the young Master? When he finally fell asleep, his dreams were a confused pantomime playing out various weird scenarios bleeding into each other and leading his mind round and round in a maze of possibilities.

Each time he woke from a dream he dropped back into another until he woke at dawn and gave up on peaceful sleep.

He pulled on his boots and quietly left the loft to George.

SEVENTEEN

The hall was in utter turmoil. The Master and his family had arrived home tired and tetchy after a long journey from France. Alice had no time to dwell on her daughter's disappearance. The staff thought it was time to turn their attention to things closer to home, such as their livelihoods. Cook made allowances for her distraction while Mr Evans almost tiptoed around her.

After the morning breakfast rush for the family, the staff, and the lunches were in hand, Alice took a tray of tea and homemade scones through to the Butler's pantry. Owen Evans stood up from his armchair and politely took the heavy tray from her.

'Thank you, Alice. Are you staying?' There were two cups on the tray making the question unnecessary. She had been taking morning tea with him most days for six months. Owen gently proffered her usual seat by the highly polished side table. He kept the room as neat and tidy as a proud housewife. Each piece of furniture is kept in a precise place. Dust never settled on the spotless surfaces and only a tiny light penetrated through the heavy velvet curtains. The strong summer sun had no chance to fade the fine fabrics and woods. The fireplace lay ready to light if the evening turned cold. The dark chilly room may have echoed his demeanour to the outsider, but Alice knew him to be a warm, caring, and thoughtful gentleman.

He poured the tea into the plain white china cups.

'Are you feeling all right, Alice?' He asked her. She nodded as he handed her the cup.

'She's on my mind constantly but I can't do anymore, and I can't ask any more of anyone. They have all been particularly good, but things must get back to the way they were. I am very worried Owen. I know she can be a little wild, but this is so unlike her.'

'Could she have run off with someone?' He did not know the child; she was a mere kitchen maid even though she was Alice's sister.

'Who? She only had us.'

'You said yourself she was wild, and she often wandered off on her own.'

'No, I'd know. A Mo... woman knows these things.' The cup clattered onto the saucer as she spoke. 'Sisters are very close, Owen.'

'You have surpassed yourself with these scones, Alice, the best yet.' He nibbled at the pastry delicately.

'Thank you.' She replied.

'This may not be the best time to discuss this Alice, however, I do think that we might look to the future. I'm sure that the Master will give his blessing.'

He walked slowly about the room; his hands clasped behind his back. He had never been an eloquent man and found it difficult to express himself on an important matter such as this. His feelings for the young woman who now sat in his company had grown over the years. He had watched her develop from a shy, timid child into the confident woman who kept the kitchen staff in order so that Cook could rule.

'It is time that I made my feelings for you clear. You know that my prospects are good, as your own are. The master will no doubt expect us to stay in his service.' He moved closer but remained standing, his back straight, his head bent slightly in order that he may see her reaction.

'You know what I am asking of you Alice. I wish to marry

you.' Her face showed no surprise at the proposal. Although he was fifteen years her senior, he was still a handsome man with a gentle nature and a good match for any woman. The seconds ticked on as Alice considered her reply. Owen made a small impatient noise in his throat brought about by nerves. 'I expect you will need time to consider your answer Alice so I will not press for your reply until such time as you think fit. However, I must say that it is a good match for all.'

'Do sit down Owen, I hate it when you pace about.' He did as she asked and sat on a near high-backed chair.

If she were to refuse him, he hoped that she would do so without delay, he was unused to feeling nervous, but this beautiful creature always made his heart pound so fast in his chest and he longed for the sight of her. The arrival of a tall and very handsome man from her past spurred him on to make this hasty proposal. He vowed to remain a bachelor, but he would break that vow for her and if she were to refuse, then his heart would surely falter.

'Please understand Owen that with everything happening I cannot make such a decision.' She took his hand and gently stroked his fingers. 'You are my dear friend and I know that you will make a good husband, but I must be sure of my feelings and not rush into marriage. I have no parents whom I can go to for guidance so I must talk to my brothers.' She was stalling for time. She could marry whom she wished, and she knew that, but did she really wish to marry Owen? He was good company and kind to her and Flo, but he did not know about her past.

She had never felt at ease enough to divulge her upbringing. If she thought so much about him, why did she not tell him about Flo? No one in the household knew Flo was not her sister but her daughter. If she were to marry Owen, he would have to know, and this frightened her. She would never marry him without him knowing the truth, but she also knew that if he knew the truth, he would surely withdraw the proposal. His strict chapel upbringing would dictate it. How to deny him without hurting him she did not know.

Owen kissed the back of her hand and they continued with the morning tea.

* * *

All eyes were on Charles when he a member of the outside staff showed him into the kitchen. Young eyelashes fluttered and cheeks flushed as he greeted the housemaids. Now the Master was back in residence and the house fully staffed, the girls had not seen the handsome friend of Alice's before.

'Take no notice of this lot Mr Bingham. Is it Alice you're looking for?' More giggles and nudges among the maids caused the Cook to turn and clap her hands. 'Get on with what you're doing and stop gawping. Sorry, Mr Bingham please take a seat and I'll fetch her for you.'

A tall willowy plain woman with bloodshot eyes and a droopy expression stepped forward as Cook called her name. 'Moll, go and tell Alice that she has a visitor. She's still with Mr Evans. She always has her morning tea with Mr Evans.' Cook told Charles.

Moll cast Charles a steely unwelcome glance as she passed him to find the assistant cook. Her face hardened further as she entered the long corridor which led to the Butler's pantry. She didn't like Alice or her spoilt brat of a crippled sister. If she had her way, the pair of them would go, out for good or out on the street. Jumped up tart that she was, played little miss innocent with all of them. If she was so good and well brought up la-de-dah, why was she sucking up to old Po-face Evans? Those brothers of hers were no more than farm labourers, dragged away from their mam to slave on the miserable Cooper farm.

Moll slowly walked down the long dark corridor pulling faces of scorn. The stone floor and walls amplified the voices from the kitchen which grew quieter as she neared the cellar door.

The door of the Butler's pantry was open as usual, for

propriety, and Mr Evans's deep Welsh voice echoed out into the corridor and to Moll's ears.

'I hope you will consider the proposal seriously Alice.' Moll did not hear Alice reply. The solid oak door swung open further as she knocked her knuckles against it. She saw Alice sitting at the table sipping her tea.

'Smarmy cow.' She thought. Mr Evans stood by the small window set deep in the solid stone. Even in the dim light, Moll saw a flush on Alice's cheeks.

'Sorry to interrupt Mr Evans but Alice has a visitor. That tall handsome chap with the charm to match.' Moll knew that had cut up the stiff-necked prig.

'It seems your brother has called on you Alice.' He smiled down at her trying not to look at the intruder.

'No Mr Evans, not her brother.' She placed emphasis on the words as much as she dared. 'That chap from America, Mr Bingham.' She didn't wait for the butler to dismiss her. The self-satisfied smirk carried her back up the corridor. Just a flicker of emotion in his eyes Moll had seen, and it had made her day. There was no way that sour puss could compete with Charlie boy. She should know; she had succumbed to those charms herself a long time ago when she had her looks.

Alice and Charles Bingham sat in the kitchen garden, the neatly trimmed privet bushes offering them privacy.

'How have you been Alice?' It was a lame question, but he did not know how to break down the barrier between them whenever they met.

'Life and work must go on Geordie. My Flo is out there somewhere hurt and frightened, and I should be with her.' He hung his head in sympathy for her. 'Do you remember when the boys ran away?'

'Aye, I only found out yesterday what became of them.'

'You've spoken to them!' Her surprise was genuine.

'Don't sound too surprised Alice. We were all out there looking for Flo. They are two great lads.'

'I worried for days over them and all the time our Cissy

and Mrs Harvey had spirited them away to the Coopers Farm. A guardian angel has helped Flo, who knows?' He took hold of her small cold hand.

'Alice, have you seen the sketches?' She nodded and tears welled in her eyes. She had looked at them repeatedly, partly distressed and a little confused about what they suggested.

'I knew she had been unwell, but I never guessed the truth of the matter. Who would do that to her? She's out there with a child and too scared to come home, isn't she?'

'You have no idea whom she was seeing?' It was obvious that she had not confided in Alice who sighed heavily in her reply.

'She was always going off on her own. I know I should have been stricter, but to tell you the truth I was glad she was out in the fresh air. So many years trapped in that awful hovel, longing to run and play took my childhood. I wanted her to be happy and free, as I never was. Is that wrong? To want your children to have what we never could?'

'What about the young man in her book?'

'Young master David! He helped her when we first came here. He encouraged her to draw and even supplied her with paper and pencils from the schoolroom. Flo missed him when he went off to school.'

'How close were they Alice?' His voice was low, a whisper.

'What are you suggesting?' Her voice raised in anger at the insinuation. 'Don't put him in the same class as your dock mates. He is a gentleman; he treats her with kindness and a little pity for her affliction that's all.'

'But he is older than her and boys, no matter what the standing, are still boys.' She shook her head vigorously.

'No, I could not believe that of him.' He was annoyed at her innocence. He had been about to tell her of her brother's macabre find and the trip to the police, but he decided against it. How would that knowledge help her? It would only make her worry more about her daughter's safety. No, it was better that she did not know. He could never steal away her hopes for Flo's safe return.

'We will just have to find her and ask.' He stated.

'Do you think we will?' She needed that hope to get through.

'Yes, I won't rest until we do.' Alice smiled weakly at him. She wanted to believe that her daughter was safe, but she secretly had her doubts. He sat quietly beside her, a comforting arm around her shoulders. She felt at ease with him. There was no sign of the old Geordie, he was Charles Bingham her dear friend and she liked being with him.

Watching the couple from the library window Owen Evans realised that he had left his marriage proposal too late. Why didn't he take the step years ago when he first realised that he loved her? Now he was certain he would lose her to the tall handsome stranger.

Another pair of eyes was also watching from her hiding place behind the garden wall. Moll's thoughts were more vengeful. He hadn't remembered her, but she would never forget him. No matter how he altered his outward appearance she would always see the real Geordie. He was still the no-good tramp, odd jobbing his way around the country. When he left her all those years ago, promising he would return he didn't know or didn't care in what state he had left her. Her father had beaten her severely while her mother watched on emotionless.

The weeks she had spent locked up in the draughty shed, sat only a few feet from the midden, had seemed like a lifetime.

Her cries for help went ignored, and the stories that she was infectious with fever kept the neighbours well out of the way. A heartless midwife had dragged the baby from her womb and taken it away. She had not seen the infant or even discover who had taken it. All because of that big fella with the charm that could talk the birds from the trees. Now he was back, not for her, but for that skinny big-eyed piece the whole house thought so much of. What was it that Alice the Angel had that was so special? Her own figure was once so trim and her skin smooth.

She had just past her thirty-fifth birthday, but she felt and looked fifty. As she watched them talking like old friends, the venom and hatred rose into her throat threatening to burn out what remained of her heart. She would have her day with them both and very soon.

* * *

Charles took his leave from Alice.

'I'll be in Stokesley for a couple of days I think, but I hope we will talk some more when I return. There is so much more that I wish to say. Be brave Alice and do not fret about Flo, I will find her. I won't rest until I do.' He wished he could take her into his arms and kiss her but that would spoil everything. If he were to make her his, he would have to first gain her complete trust.

Alice watched him walk away. He had a confident swagger, his dust coat swaying about him in unison with his walk. The large hat beat against his thighs as he made his way to his horse and out of her sight. She thought momentarily about what life would have been like had she stayed with him. Had she really disliked him that much or was it the events that had surrounded them? He stirred feelings of a different kind in her now.

Feelings that she did not understand. They had never even been friends; how could she feel anything for him now? Perhaps because he knew where her roots lie, they had things in common and similar backgrounds. It would be necessary to give Owen an answer to his proposal. How would she reply? She thought very highly of him, but she doubted that there was any love in her relationship with him. They had been friends for a long time, and she did feel comfortable in his company, but was that enough to base a marriage on? If Flo had not disappeared, would she have hesitated over her answer? Or was it the arrival of a face from the past that had made her ambivalent? She rubbed her hands over her face as if trying to wipe away her misgivings then she returned to the kitchen and to her work.

.

EIGHTEEN

The market town of Stokesley opened out before him. The sun was high and hot, the coaching inns beckoned with a cool beer to quench his thirst. He would stop for a bite to eat before reporting Flo's disappearance. He didn't believe they could do very much but there was always a chance that she may have already returned home. An eager young groom ran towards him.

'I'll take yer horse sir if yer care to take a rest.' Charles gladly handed the reins to the youth then turned towards the Sun Inn. Before he reached the doorway, another eager body closed in on him and a grubby gnarled hand thrust toward him.

'Spare a copper. I'm sure a fine gentleman like yourself can take pity on a man down on his luck and wish him well.' Charles stepped back away from the stench emanating from the tramp. The smell was enough to knock a strong man over. 'Sorry, you can see I'm in need of a bath, I've been on the road a long time.'

'It's a bit more than a wash you need man.' Charles wafted his hand around his nose to breath fresh air.

'I don't believe me ears.' The tramp looked up into the big man's face. 'It is you, isn't it? Geordie, big Geordie.' Charles glared down in condemnation at Bert. 'I'd know that voice anywhere, but I'd never have known you in that getup. By you've done well for yersel'.' Bert fingered the fine cloth of Charles's coat. Charles brushed the dirty hand away.

'I never thought I would see you again after the business with your wife. I'd have thought you would have left the country or at least the area.' It was hard to believe that of all people he could casually meet it could be Alice's father. It was incredulous that the fool would still be in the area where he had committed his crime.

'I did. Well, I left the area. I went down Norfolk way, and had quite a good life for a while. Couldn't settle though but look at you!' He exclaimed.

'Never mind me.' Once more Charles had to knock the old man's hands away. He knew too well how fast those fingers could lift a wallet.

'Buy us a beer mate for old times Eh, 'Ere I might 'ave summit that'll take yer fancy.' Bert stepped to one side and grabbed at the girl who sat at his feet. 'Look, she's clean 'n worth paying for eh.' He dragged Flo to her feet and shoved her towards Charles who grabbed her arms to stop her from falling.

'She's exhausted,' Charles said. The girl was pale, almost waxen. Her eyes were black with deep dark shadows and a cut lip encrusted with blood and dirt.

'Who is she? Why is she with you?' Bert looked pleased with himself because Charles was showing an interest in his find.

'You like her then? She's mine.' His crooked grin showed his blackened nicotine-stained teeth.

'What do you mean, she's yours? Talk sense man.'

'I found her she's mine. Can't you see?' He grabbed at her face forcing her pale cheeks into her clenched teeth. 'She's never opened her mouth for days except to eat. Struck dumb at meeting her old man I guess.' The realisation hit Charles like a kick from an unbroken colt, his stomach churned, and his mouth became dry. He wiped his hand over his mouth such was the sickly feeling that he felt. 'This is Flo, Alice's daughter?'

'Aye, like I said she's mine.'

'You, filthy bastard.' His fist hit Bert square in the jaw knocking him off his feet. 'Get up.' Charles roared at the prone

149

figure. 'So, I can hit you again you dirty pock-ridden leach.' Bert tried to crawl away, but his assailant had a tight grip on the tramp's ragged coat. Flo, seeing her chance sprang away like a frightened fawn.

She had no idea what was happening, but it was her one opportunity to get away and she did not hesitate.

'Flo!' Charles called after her, leaving hold of his grip on Bert's coat long enough for the old man to make his escape. The girl disappeared around a corner. He turned back to Bert in time to see him running as fast as his crooked legs could carry him in the opposite direction. 'Oh, Bloody hell!' He exclaimed.

A small crowd of men had gathered in the hope of seeing a fistfight. They each now shrugged their shoulders and began to disperse blocking Charles's view of the route Bert took. He decided that it was more important to follow the girl, but he soon realised that she had gone.

'Poor lass.' He thought. 'She must be terrified.' He stood for a moment on the stone bridge looking downriver.

Away in the distance, he saw the distinctive figure of a smelly crippled tramp sneaking behind a row of neat cottages. Determined to catch the murderous rogue, he ran back to the stable yard to collect his horse. In the yard, to his amazement, he saw Flo with the stable boy. He had her pinned against the wall slapping her face. She slumped down the wall sobbing, and he kicked her in the ribs. Charles ran across the yard in four strides and grabbed the boy by the scruff, his long hair caught in Charles's fingers so he could not wriggle free.

'Get off.' The youth screamed. Charles pushed the boy into the same wall which moments ago he had pinned Flo against. He seized the boy's arm and forced it up his back, the other hand still pushing the lad's red, angry face into the stone wall.

'Why were you hurting the girl?' Charles said calmly.

'Please don't hurt me. She's nowt, honest just a street whore.' Charles jabbed the youth's body into the wall.

'I happen to know that she is not, so I'll ask you again. Why were you hitting her?'

'She came at me first mister. honest. She kicked me an' was making noises. She's a bit simple.' Charles growled in the lad's ear.

'She's deaf, but she's not daft.' He spun the boy round, their faces now only inches away. 'Now, tell me who you are and what that girl is to you.' Charles shook the boy by the front of the dirty shirt.

'All right, Mister, all right I'll tell yer'.' The grip relaxed a little. "Er name's Flo, works out at Ayton in the big house. I used help in the stables an' we were friends, sort of.' He paused. 'She had a baby in an old loft. I found her there, but the baby was already dead. It was. there was blood everywhere.' He pointed towards the distraught figure crouched on the yard floor. 'She thought it was my fault but how am I supposed to know, I mean she could've been with anyone couldn't she? But I never 'urt it or her honest

'What's your name lad?' Charles spat the question.

'Adam, Adam Porter.'

'Well Adam Porter, I'd like to know how you came to be here?'

'I ran away after I saw her in that loft. I've only been here a couple of days,' terrified of what this huge man might do.

'I know that girl and her family and if she thinks you were to blame for her plight then I must believe her.' Adam, the stable boy shook his head denying that it had been his fault. 'However, I also believe you when you say the child was stillborn.' The lad visibly relaxed. 'I would suggest that the best thing you could do right now is to get out of my sight because if
I ever lay eyes on you again; I will not be responsible for my actions.' He threw the boy away from him with such force that the youngster staggered to remain on his feet, crashing against the yard wall as he made his escape. Just at that moment, the Innkeeper stepped into the yard.

'Ere what's going on out 'ere? And where does he think 'e's going?'

'You will be needing a new stable lad, that one is not of

good character.' Charles bent down to the curled-up figure of Flo. He took her face in his huge hands.

'Flo. Flo, I am a friend of Alice and I have come to help you. She sent me to find you.' Her dirty tear-stained face looked back at him blankly. How was he to know if she understood? Alice never told him how to make her understand. 'I won't hurt you.' He mouthed slowly but there was still no response. The proprietor moved closer to them.

'Can I help?' He asked.

'Yes, you can. If you have a room for her to rest while I see to other business. If your wife would give her a bath and tend to her, I would be grateful?'

'I have no wife Sir, but my daughter will oblige the young lass. Bring her in.' He left the girl in the safe hands of the innkeeper and his daughter, and in the absence of Adam the stable boy he saddled his horse and rode off in the direction he had last seen Bert.

* * *

The old man kept to the riverbank, he felt it would be better to stay well out of sight while making his escape from the madman that used to be his friend. What could have turned the Big Geordie into a soft touch like that? They had been such good drinking partners for years. Hadn't he taken the boy from Newcastle under his wing when he first arrived at the docks? He was only a lanky kid then, about the same age as Alice, or a bit older, he had been tall for his age even then. He had also been a quick learner; he soon knew all the tricks and dodges of the docks. Now it seems that the big Newcastle docker who had once been on the run from the law for attempted murder babysat stupid girls.

The ground under his feet was wet and marshy making his progress slow and hazardous. Higher up the bank, the bushes were thickening so he clambered towards their cover.

'Damn!' He swore as his ragged coat caught on a bramble, tearing the hole in his pocket further, and spilling the contents among the long grass. A rush of blood hit his head as he bent to retrieve his belongings.

The pain pulsated behind his eyes, sharp needles burning into every nerve. His bruised face was now hot and inflamed, bright lights lit up his sight even though he had closed his eyes momentarily. He staggered and almost fell forward but managed to sit back onto the ground. After a moment, he placed his few treasures, a couple of coppers and cigarette stubs of various lengths, into the ragged bag he had taken from the river when he had first noticed Flo.

He dragged himself to his feet with the aid of an overhanging tree branch and walked three yards before he needed to rest again. His head pounded, and he felt sick. Suddenly he was extremely hot, and the sweat beads on his forehead gathered into pools before trickling down his temples. With a huge effort he removed his coat, the pots and pans clattered as he threw it to the ground.

Slowly he crawled back towards the river hoping to quench the thirst which now raged in his throat. As he reached over the bank with his hand cupped to take the water, a pain hit his chest. It had a force that was far harder than any punch Big Geordie could have thrown. A tingling sensation crept down his left arm, he tried to get to his feet, but the ground was too soft and muddy. The pain in his chest hit again like a docker's boot taking another kick in a street brawl. His head felt as if it were about to explode. He fell backwards into the cool water. He was dead before the water covered his face.

❊ ❊ ❊

Charles looked down on the pain-contorted face of the dead tramp. The daylight was fading behind the distant hills by the time he had noticed Bert's discarded belongings in the undergrowth. He jumped down from his horse and followed the trail through the mud and grass. Bert lay dead, his body splayed among the shale and rocks on the river's edge. The bruising on his face showed more obvious against the death pallor of his skin. With a gloved hand, Charles rubbed his own unshaven face.

'Did I kill him?' He thought. Was the blow he dealt him enough to lay him that low? He had been furious when he threw that punch. Anger for Bert's treatment of Flo, and Alice. Oh! Yes. The more he thought about Bert's past, the less he cared that the scoundrel lay dead by his hand. He is just another tramp living rough. No one will either know or care who he was or how he met his death.

With that thought, he instantly searched Bert's pockets. There was nothing to give away the identity of the body. Among the scattered belongings, Charles spotted a cloth bag. Curious he bent to inspect it closer, it had to be a lady's bag. It was quite large, about a foot square, and the handles were long and broad. The fabric was grubby and well-worn, but it was still possible to see that it had been a fine item. He felt the texture between his fingers, there were beads still attached and the quilting still stood proud in places. He flung the bag over his horse before climbing into the saddle and making his way back to the inn and to Flo.

NINETEEN

The funeral had been large and very well attended. Everyone in the area paid their respects to their dear friend and neighbour. After a lengthy illness, Tess Harvey died quietly in her sleep.

Cissy sat reading beside the bed waiting for the inevitable. When she thought her guardian was asleep, she rested her own head on the back of the finely upholstered chair and slept. When she woke, she realised that the frail old lady, who not only had been a dear friend but also the mother she needed had died.

People sat downstairs in the small parlour eating small bite-size sandwiches and fancy cakes, talking about how poor Tess had suffered and what a wonderful person she had been. 'Wasn't it a shame she had no family to speak of, and how would sweet Cissy cope without her guardian. The poor child was past consoling.' Mrs Wrightson said to a group of mourners.

She was upstairs in the same room that she had spent months nursing Tess through each stroke until a weak heart had given up the struggle to beat in the emaciated chest. She looked out of the window onto the same view she had looked out at all these years. She knew every brick of the old derelict cottages opposite. Hopefully, all the filthy hovels would soon be gone taking with them her despicable childhood.

'Are you all right Cissy?' Her brother Joe called from the bedroom door before entering. She nodded but did not turn around to face him. 'Everyone has gone. Agnes is just clearing away the last of the dishes. Won't you come down?' He had loved the dear old soul as well as his sister. She had been kind and generous to the Allertons.

He had admired and respected her for years after she had spirited the two lads away and then taken Cissy on. Poor Tess had been good to him and

Agnes, always gave the children little treats.

'I'm all right Joe, please don't fuss. I'll be down in a minute.' He walked to his sister's side and glanced out of the window, curious to see what was holding her attention.

'It's not a pretty sight is it Cissy?' He said, 'There's talk of it coming down.'

'Yes, I'd heard that. Do you ever think back to those days Joe?'

'Not if I can help it I don't, they're not the best of memories are they? I can only remember how miserable it was,' he said.

'You were all right, you are a boy.'

'Not really. I wasn't. I watched how Dad went at Mam and then he started on Alice. You were too young to know or understand all of it. I had a hard job trying to understand it myself. I couldn't wait to get away from it all. If I had stayed, who knows how things might have turned out? Alice got you over here because she was afraid of what might become of you.'

'I realised that Joe. Tess took loving care of me and gave me a good start but...' She hesitated.

'But what Cissy?'

'The last few years I have felt as trapped as Alice must have done. I do not mean to be ungrateful because I am not. I know I would have been worse off if I had stayed over there.' She pointed to the derelict cottages. 'Tess was a kind and wonderful friend and I miss her so much, but I made a big sacrifice to stay with her Joe and now I'm alone and an Old Maid.'

'Don't talk daft our Cissy you are not old nor are you alone. Tess left you well provided; she left you everything. My but she was a dark horse eh! No one would have guessed that she owned half the street and two shops. Why did she stay in this old place when she had a choice? She could have lived anywhere.' Cissy smiled knowingly at her brother.

'Tess loved it round here. Everyone thought the world of her. If folk had known how wealthy her husband had left her, they may have shunned her or worse, asked too many favours.'
'Yeh I can see that happening. What will you do now?
Are you going to move on?'

'Where would I go, I don't know anything else?'

'Alice did it!'

'She had her reasons; she could see herself becoming like Mam if she'd stayed. No, I'll stay on here for a while.' She pondered.

'He won't come back now you know.' He had read her thoughts. If she was holding out hopes for Mathew's return, she was heading for disappointment.

'I know, but there must be a reason for all this. To suddenly have more than I need or want, I just cannot see it yet, but one day it will be clear.
Come on Joe let us have tea.' She led the way down the narrow stairs of the 'two up, two down' townhouse, one that she now owned and the other nine in the street.

❋ ❋ ❋

'Someone's been in my room,' Alice said to Cook.

'Are you sure pet?' Cook looked at Alice over the top of her account book. The monthly accounts had to be ready for inspection by Mr Evans.

'Everything has been moved but I don't think there is anything missing.'

'Has Jane been in to clean?'

'No. I always do my own room. You don't think that

maybe...?'

'If you're thinking Flo might have been in there then think again lass. She could never have sneaked in past the staff. Not today, while there are so many of them about. Anyway, she moved out of your room ages ago why would she need to go in now?'

'You're right, but someone has been in there I'm sure of it.' Alice shrugged her shoulders and poured the hot milk she had been standing over into the two cups. They sat together companionably at the fire drinking their hot milk. The rest of the staff had retired early as they would have to be up at dawn.

'When's your friend calling back?' Cook asked Alice who frowned questionably.

'Oh, you mean Mr Bingham.'

'You know fine well whom I mean.'

'I'm not sure. He went into Stokesley on business this morning. He said he might be away for a couple of days.'

'He's nice, I like him. If I were twenty years younger, I might have run off with him.' Alice flapped her hand at her old friend.

'He's just a friend Cook. An old friend from a long time ago.' Her face was warm with a blush, but in the dim light the cook did not see her embarrassment

'I think he has come back for you. And it is not a friend he has come back for neither.' Cook winked. Alice lowered her head but did not reply.

With the finished accounts tucked under his arm, Owen Evans marched towards the kitchen to return Cook's volume.

The busy kitchen was noisier than usual and as he pushed open the door it was obvious why. Moll and Alice stood face to face glowering like street fighters preparing to scrap. Cook stood beside the two sparing women, her arms crossed under her ample bosom.

The rest of the staff stood around the two women egging them on to fight.

'You took it from my room,' Alice shouted at Moll. 'Give it back or else...' Moll was waving a sheet of paper around out of Alice's grasp.

'I think everyone should see what it is first.' Her tone was mocking and childish.

'Don't you dare? It's private.' Alice tried once more to reach the paper, but Moll was five or six inches taller.

'You can't draw pictures like this and not show them.' Moll was enjoying the game. 'Look girls there's a picture of Evans's old frosty face.'

As she spoke the words, she noticed the butler in the doorway, the other girls had already seen him enter and quietened. Alice spun around at the sound of the stern voice.

'I would like to see what all the fuss is about.' Everyone in the room stood still and silent. Mr Evans walked slowly into the room and toward the two women. Moll dropped her arm the paper hung loosely at waist height. When he held out his hand, she obediently placed the drawing into the short square immaculately manicured hand.

There was utter silence in the kitchen and all eyes were on the butler as he perused the various drawings on the paper. His eyebrows raised slightly, but he showed no other emotion. After what seemed like an hour yet was only ten seconds he spoke.

'I think I deserve an explanation.' He looked across at Cook. 'What's going on Mrs Ford?'

'Moll has been in Alice's room Mr Evans, which I think you will agree is very disrespectful and she is now taking immense pleasure in upsetting the whole place. I have no idea what has gotten into her, but I will tell you one thing I know for sure and that is Moll has it in for poor Alice. She's wicked that girl.' He looked over to the two women who had been causing such a racket. The withering looks spurred Moll into a verbal outburst.

'She's such a goody-two-shoes, I wanted to find out what she had that I don't.' Moll's high-pitched whining voice grated on his fine hearing.

'That is not the explanation I was expecting.' He closed

his eyes against the crude voice. Alice spoke next.

'You shouldn't be looking through my room and taking my personal things.'

'I don't see why not, how else is anyone gonna find out what yer hiding in there? We might even 'ave found out why yer sister ran away.' She stood with her hands on her hips leaning into Alice's face menacingly.

'Flo did not run away.' Alice bellowed in retaliation.

'You had no right Moll to pry into the personal belongings of ANY of the staff, whether high or low. I do not take it upon myself to raid your room periodically nor would any other member of the staff.'

'I just looked around Mr Evans; I didn't take anything except these daft bits of paper honest.' Moll stood with her chin on her chest and her hands deep in the apron pockets. 'Ask 'er what's she doing with a load of silver hidden away, It's not her's. It has a posh crest on it. You don't know half of what I've found out about her. She's just a jumped-up nowt from the back streets. All her high and mighty ways she's no better than a kitchen scrubber. I know people in Middlesbrough who know you and your stinking thieving dad. Oh! You need to look shocked Alice Allerton, but my Mam has worked with a certain Sally Allerton an' she loves to talk about YOU.' She folded her arms dramatically hitching her small bosom as she did so. Alice stared at the maid in disbelief. 'Oh yes, she doesn't like you at all, yer own sister.' Moll had everyone's attention. 'Your Sal told my Mam about how yer sent her away into service, just a bairn she was, while you were laying with yer own dad.' Cook took a sharp intake of breath.

Alice sat with a thud on the nearby chair she could not deny Moll's words because in the eyes of her poor younger sister that must have been how she had seen those sad events of their childhood.

'See.' Moll pointed to the stricken figure on the chair. 'She knows I'm right.' Alice swallowed hard before replying.

'No Moll, you are not right, yes Sal was very young when she went away, but it was for her own good.' All eyes were now on the assistant cook. 'My father had Sally lined up when he had finished with me.' Moll interrupted.

'That's not the way she saw it. She said that yer Mam was always drunk and cried a lot, and you and yer brothers sent the youngsters out to beg.' This was too much for Alice to bear. She drew on her hidden strength and stood to face Moll, having to look up into the red bloated face of her angry opponent.

'Now you just stop there.' A fist waved menacingly in Moll's face. 'Our Sal would never have said those things.'

'Are you saying my Mam's telling lies?' Alice shook her head slowly and determinedly.

'No Moll, I'm saying you are making all this up out of a tiny snippet of gossip. Yes, my father used me because my mother was ill, but she was not a drunk. And my brothers and sisters did not beg. I worked extremely hard to keep the family together, Sal had to go into service for her own safety.' Moll took up the challenge.

'But yer dad is still a thief and yer Mam's daft, and Sal says Flo's not yer sister, she's yours.' She pushed at Alice's shoulder sending her off balance and back onto the wooden chair. For a moment Alice was unable to answer. She glanced up into the bewildered face of Owen, the man who had just recently proposed marriage to her. That would never happen now, not now he knew the truth. Her voice a whisper she said, whilst still looking directly at Owen.

'Yes, all right, I will not deny that Flo is my daughter, but I have never lied because no one has asked me. You all just assumed she was my sister, and I did not correct you.' Cook looked hurt.

'You could have told me, Lass, I thought you were my friend?' Alice looked despairingly at the matronly woman she had always confided in.

'I couldn't Cook. I didn't want anyone to know about my past. I made a new life for myself when my mother died.' She looked up at the shocked faces staring back at her. 'I'll save you from Moll's gossip and tell you now that my mother was murdered by my father.'

'I think this has gone far enough.' Owen Evans pushed Moll away from Alice and waved his arms in dismissal of the rest of the staff. 'I will speak to you later Moll. You have still intruded into her room and must bear the consequence. All of you get on with your work.' He looked down at Alice but could not speak to her. He needed time to absorb the information this woman had just released. This was not the Alice he had proposed to; she had been a lovely gentle creature, with poise and grace.

He imagined her raised up a lady, poor perhaps but with a happy family such as his own upbringing. To discover that her own father brutally raped her and her mother a lunatic was beyond his comprehension. He knew that such things occurred, he was not that innocent. He could not see Alice's bravery in escaping from the situation or her tenacity and strength which kept her siblings safe. Even if he had known the whole story, he would still have held the same opinion.

Cook placed a cup of tea in front of Alice.

'Get that into you Pet.' She glowered at Mr Evans who stood stone still looking down at Alice. At that moment there was a knock at the heavy oak door and Charles Bingham entered. Moll followed behind him and as if introducing him shouted.

'Look what's just dragged itself here! Just to top it off.' She sneered. Cook yelled back at her.

'You were told to get on with your work, now please do so.' Moll pulled an unsavoury face at the old woman and appeared to leave the kitchen, but she stayed within hearing distance. Just outside the kitchen door.

Charles saw at once that Alice was suffering distress. He went to her side, and Owen stepped away avoiding any contact with him. This man whom he considered his rival for Alice. On his knees in front of Alice Charles took her hand in his and stroked her fingers.

'I've some good news for you Alice, Flo has been found.'

'Thank the good Lord for that.' She looked at his face, so close to hers that she felt his warm breath on her cheek. 'Is she safe Charles?'

'Yes, love she is safe. I've left her at the Coopers Farm.'

'Best place for the little slut.' Moll could not contain herself behind the door anymore, she was determined to make Alice and the big Geordie lout regret they ever met her. Charles looked over his shoulder at the intruder. Cook left the bread she had been busy kneading and with a flowery fist threatened Moll.

'I'm not going to put up with any more of your nonsense Moll.' Moll brushed Cook's arm aside as she pushed through to reach Alice and Charles. Owen suddenly came to his senses and placed himself between the troublesome Moll and her target.

'Leave it, Moll, you have done enough damage for one day.'

'What on earth is going on here?' Charles stood up behind Owen Evans, towering over the short butler.

'We've all been finding out about Alice Allerton here and I think they might like to know more about you.' Moll was determined to have her say. Alice pushed Charles and Owen to one side and faced her tormentor.

'You can keep your silly gossip to yourself, Molly Smith. You know nothing about Geordie.'

'Oh, I know him better than you think.' Moll pointed at the man in question. 'You pretend you don't remember me, but you just think back. I was prettier back then, of course, and a lot younger and stupid enough to believe that you loved me.' All eyes were now on Charles, including the kitchen girls giggling in the comer at the unexpected entertainment.

'Be careful Moll,' Charles said quietly, 'you are about to hurt nobody but yourself. I remember you very well, but I thought you didn't want to know me as I treated you so badly.' He turned the tables on her as diplomatically as he could without giving too much away. 'I also was very young then and I know I let you down dreadfully but that is in the past.' He had walked towards her his arms held out in a caring pose. 'Can we talk alone Moll?' She backed away from him suspicious of his motives.

'You stay away from me, or else.' Moll was now unsure of herself. Her face began to crumble, and tears stung her eyes. 'Go and see to your precious Alice and leave me alone I...I have work to do.' She scuttled out of the kitchen without looking back at the faces staring in her direction. 'Let them think what they like. She thought, she knew she was right, Alice and Flo were nothing, but trollops and he was no better. They were not going to get away with it. None of them was, she would see to all of them.

'What was all that about?' Alice took hold of Charles' arm. He turned to look at her and shrugging his shoulders he answered.

'Goodness knows?' He led her back to the chair. Cook clapped her hands, scattering clouds of flour into the air, ushering the staff back to their duties.

Owen Evans excused himself and quietly walked to his pantry. He had no idea what to do. His entire world was upside down, and his plans to marry Alice were no longer possible. But how could he face her every day now he knew her circumstances.? Would she expect him to stand by his proposal? Could he live with the truth of her past? It would have been easier if she had been honest with him from the start. He did not want to lose her to Mr Bingham, but he already had. Maybe if they had a fresh start somewhere else, back in Wales? Yes, that was the answer. He would give it more thought before he spoke to her again. He must also remember to ask her about the remark Moll had made about Alice having silver.

❅ ❅ ❅

At the end of a long and tiring and eventful day, Alice and Charles sat on the flat cart and drove slowly towards Cooper's farm for a reunion with Flo. Moll stayed out of the way for the rest of the day and the subject of Alice's past had not risen again. Few words passed between the couple until they were at the farm gates when Charles spoke first.

'Flo will be pleased to see you.'

'I actually don't believe that Charles.' Her voice was sad and despondent.

'Why ever not?'

'She doesn't like me very much and probably thinks that I'm going to punish her for the trouble she has caused. I've always been the one who had to discipline her.' The cart juddered and shook as the wheels caught in the dried wheel tracks of the rough track leading to the farm. 'I have tried so hard with her, hard. When I was learning how to talk to her, I had to take her face in my hands and hold her so tight so that she would not pull away. It used to leave red marks on her face. She would hit me and pull at my hair till I let her go. I have never had any affection from her, no kisses or hugs; she rarely even smiled at me. If she were naughty, I would shake her so hard, I could not hit her. Mrs Samuelson, the boss's wife who was teaching me to bake, she could get through to Flo.'

Charles slowed the cart, Alice needed to talk, and he was there to listen.

'Flo would hug Mrs Samuelson like she was her mother and not me. I was the one who shook her and held her too tight or stopped her from doing something she wanted even if it was to stop her from hurting herself. I don't even think she knows I am her mother, I'm just Alice.' Her eyes filled with tears. Charles brought the cart to a halt several yards from the farmyard wall. He turned to look at her.

'Alice, I know that I have not been around to see her grow up, but I know that you will have done your best by her. You were only a girl when she was born, you had no time to give

her, and it must have been hard. You must not blame yourself.'
'I looked after the others and at least I know that I did all right with Cissy and Joe, and Eddie and George love me.' The tears were falling steadily now.

'Yes, but they were your brothers and sister that is different.'

'How is it different? I had to bring them all up just the same, I was on my own with Flo and I still didn't do right, did I? She ran wild on the hills till she lays with the first lad who asks.'

'You don't know that for certain Alice.'

'I know that if I had left her with Mrs Samuelson and not dragged her back up here, she would have been better off. But no, I know best, and I take her away from the one person she had grown close to. Mrs Samuelson was her mother in every way. She wanted me to leave her there, she would have taken her for her own, but I was selfish and wanted her with me.'

'You are her mother, Alice, of course, you wanted her with you.' He tried to reassure her. He put his arm around her shoulders, and she leant against him. 'None of this is your fault, Alice, you did your best. Now let us see those lanky brothers of yours and your silly wayward daughter.' He knew her feeling of guilt would not brush aside easily and soon she would have to face it again, but this was neither the time nor the place.

❋ ❋ ❋

Charles sat at the kitchen table of Cooper's farm with Eddie and George. He told them how he had found her with their father in Stokesley and about the stable boy who had admitted responsibility for her condition. There was a sigh of relief from Eddie who had nurtured the idea that it might have been young Master David who had taken Flo.

'So, this Adam was he the lad that had been helping in High Fell stables. How did Da get hold of her?' Eddie wondered.

'I never actually asked him.' Replied Charles. 'I was much

166

too angry to converse with the old goat.' Alice entered the kitchen.

'She was very sleepy when I went up. The sedative the doctor gave her seems to be doing its job.' Alice looked across at Charles. She had received the greeting she predicted. Flo turned her head away from her mother not wanting to see or hear what she said.

George had remained noticeably quiet during the telling of Flo's 'adventure' his face emotionless. He scrapped his chair against the stone floor as he stood and hurriedly left the kitchen. Eddie shook his head at his brother's weakness and then left to follow him.

'I don't think he ever got over finding the infant like that and then to find out that it was poor Flo's,' Charles said. Alice shuddered at the words.

'You don't think that she drowned the child do you, Charles?'

'No, I made discreet enquiries at the police station. The Doctor said it never lived. A still-birth he called it, too small to survive. Don't worry I mentioned no names. I told them I knew the chap who had found the child and was asking on his behalf. They were helpful.' He drew his gaze away from her sad face before he continued.

'I didn't want the lads to know everything, but I think you should know that your father is dead.' He glanced back at her to note her reaction. Her mouth fell open and her eyes widened. Both her hands slapped on the table as she threw herself forward towards Charles.

'How do you know? Are you sure?'

'I found him by the river laid out cold. I think I may have killed him, Alice.' Her face paled.

'What do you mean you killed him? How?' Her voice was a harsh whisper.

'When I found him with Flo and knew his intentions for her, I lashed out and punched him hard in the face. He went down like a stone, that's when Flo ran off.'

'But you said you found him by the river.' She was confused.

'Well, yes, he staggered off when I went looking for Flo.'

'Then how could you have killed him?'

'It happened once before only the chap didn't die. When I was fighting, I knocked this sailor out and I thought he was dead, and so did everyone else. Bert collapsed because I hit him so hard, he was an old man, and I shouldn't have hit him.'

'You hit him out of anger Charles you didn't mean to kill him, that's if you did. It could have been anything, as you said he was an old man.'

'Well, he's gone now and I'm certain of one thing, I'm glad that he is. He can't hurt you or Flo anymore.' Alice's brothers returned as Charles finished speaking.

'It's time I took you back to the house Alice. It'll be dark soon.'

'Eddie will take me home Charles. Please come and fetch me tomorrow afternoon so that I can talk to Flo.' Charles nodded just once, and she left with her brother.

TWENTY

'**I**'m pleased that you could find time to have morning tea with me, Alice.' Owen was pouring the tea into the delicate white cups. His companion sat quietly in the chair beside him. 'The scene in the kitchen yesterday with Moll was very unfortunate, for all of us I believe.' Alice hung her head slightly and took a deep breath, which sounded like a sigh. 'Yes, I can understand your distress however I must say that I felt terribly upset by the whole thing. Not so much the information which came out but the reality that you didn't feel able to confide in me.'

'Owen.' Alice pleaded.

'No Alice, please let me finish.' He took his usual stance, hands behind his back clasped together. 'I have had time to consider the events, and I have decided that we could still make a good marriage however I also think that we would be advised to make a fresh start elsewhere. I thought that we might return to Wales.' He looked carefully for her reaction; his eyebrows raised in anticipation of a favourable reply. Rather than looking pleased with his suggestion Alice looked quite irate.

He had never seen her like this before. She had always been so composed and genteel. She never raised her voice to anyone. Was this the real Alice coming out?

'How could you decide for me, Owen? Had you considered that, as I had not actually answered your proposal that the answer might have been negative? Yes, there were things thrown at me yesterday, Owen. It was my character Moll attacked. Oh, no doubt that it was for your behalf, she could never keep titbits like that to herself could old Moll? I did think that I could marry you Owen, but I would never have accepted your proposal without telling you the truth. I could never have kept you in ignorance of Flo's parentage.' She took a deep breath. 'Do you love me, Owen?'

'Of course, I think very highly of you Alice.'

'That's not what I asked.' She stood facing him, she could see his tight collar was almost choking him. His face was very red, either from the heat in the oppressive little room or his embarrassment. He was not a demonstrative man; he kept his emotions deep within his inner self, and even Alice could not break that wall.

'I am prepared to forgive you and take your hand in marriage; it shows how much I care for you.'

'Forgive me for what? Being raped by my own father or deceiving you?' He didn't answer her, he could not look her in the eye. She was glaring at him waiting for his response. 'Caring for me is not enough Owen, you need to understand me and know even more unpleasant facts about my past. Shall I tell you, Owen? Shall I?' He turned away from her and moved towards the window. Standing now with his back to her he sighed heavily.

'I'm sorry Alice, I do not want to sound harsh but there has been an ample amount of your past for me to embrace, I do not think I could bear any more.'

'Well, that's a shame, All I had to do was to live through it and try and get over it. I dragged myself out of that gutter of a home and with the help of two exceedingly kind people I educated myself and my daughter. We may not be up to your standard Owen, but I have worked hard to rid us of the dreadful curse of poverty. I still bear the scars and people like Moll will always find me out so there is no point in running anymore.'

'I understand Alice.'

'No Owen you don't. You never will, and that's why I delayed telling you.'

'What will you do?' He turned once more to face her, he felt calmer and more in control of the situation.

'Are you asking me to leave High Fell?'

'It will be difficult for you to stay in the light of what has been said.'

'Why? As I said I will not run away. If he will not accept me for who I am, then the Master will have to dismiss me because I will not leave any other way.' Her face was set in a determined expression, her eyes half-closed and her mouth severe.

'The family do not need to know how things are.'

'Then you will have to think of another reason for getting me pushed out for I will not leave voluntarily.'

'What about your friend Mr Bingham?' It was more of a statement than a question.

'He has nothing to do with any of this.'

'You and he are very close.'

'I have known him for a long time, and he is a very good friend.' Did she believe that? They had only just become friends really.

'Perhaps you will leave with him.' Alice shook her head in disbelief.

'Do you what me to go that badly that you would find me another suitor?' The exasperation in her voice wasted on him. He only heard the words he wished to hear. Selectively removing the phrases and the intonations that he did not wish to accept.

'Then I will put everything behind me and try to continue our working relationship in the usual way.' He walked to the door and opened it for the departing visitor. Under her breath Alice said.

'Has anyone ever told you what a selfish prig you are?' She did not expect him to answer.

'Oh, before you leave, Moll mentioned silver yesterday.

171

Can you tell me what she meant?' He barred her exit with his arm waiting for her reply. Alice pushed his arm away and as she opened the door, she spat the words.

'You couldn't possibly bear to hear any more of my sordid history, remember.' Neither of them heard the soft pad of slipped feet retreating down the stone-clad corridor.

* * *

The early evening air was oppressive; a summer storm was hanging in the air. Beads of perspiration rolled gently down her back causing a wet patch to gather where her back leant against the leather backrest of the farm's only trap. Her brother Eddie had called to take her to the farm, as Charles was busy with Mr Cooper and a horse in foal.

'They get on really well do Geordie and the Boss.' Eddie was telling her. 'He's been showing us the fancy ways he learnt in America. Don't you think he's changed, Alice? I don't remember much about him back then except that I didn't like him very much, but I like him now. Our George took to him as well, but he wouldn't say so. He is still too quiet is George. He got right upset over that little baby, more so when he knew where it had come from. Soft as clarts is George.' He looked at his passenger.

'Are you all right Alice you're very quiet?' She nodded and smiled weakly at her brother. 'Flo's brighter today. She's sat up in the kitchen by the window and had a little broth. Of course, Ma Cooper is fussing about like a mother hen. She misses having Lizzie to look after.' He chattered aimlessly for the whole fifteen-minute journey. As he helped her to alight from the well-used trap, the step was a bit rickety, and he looked into her sad eyes and said. 'It will be all right Alice everything happens for His great plan. Something bad must happen before you realise how much good there is in your life.'

'That's very profound Eddie.' She replied.

172

'Well, if I knew what that meant I might be flattered.' He joked. Before she went into the house, she gave him a quick sisterly hug.

'Thank you for the sermon, Father Edward, I will keep it in mind.'

Flo looked young and vulnerable in the huge four-poster bed. The carved and turned oak posts were quite imposing, and the heavy curtains which clothed the posts softened the look of the bed. Alice's daughter lay back on the bed her deep brown wavy hair spread out over the pillow. She was very pale and the bruises on her face showed a rainbow of colours as they slowly healed. Alice had not expected the emotional response Flo was giving at the sight of her mother.

The previous evening, she had seemed so cold and distant. The child had real tears in her eyes as they embraced. After a moment of mutual comforting Alice held her daughter at arms-length so she could read her lips. Flo did not resist.

'I have been so worried about you.' Flo nodded and in response showed her regret. 'Can you tell me anything?' Alice asked her. The young lips quivered in a childish pout, and she shook her head. Fingering the girl's bruises, she asked who it to her Flo had done simply signed.

'MAN'

'Which man?'

'OLD MAN.' According to Charles, it had been the boy who had been hitting Flo when he had found her so to get her on the right track Alice started again.

'I want you to think hard and tell me what happened.' With a personal sign language of their own, Flo told the story.

WALK. TUMMY HURT. HEAD HURT. IN BARN. SICK. TINY BABY. NO LIFE. BOY CAME. WENT AWAY. BABY RIVER. VERY SAD.

RAIN. FLO FRIGHTENED. SMELLY OLD MAN. FIRE FOOD. LONG WALK. TOWN. BIG MAN HIT OLD MAN. RAN AWAY. BOY IN YARD. HIT ME. BIG MAN CAME. WASH. SLEEP. FOOD. FARM.

She watched Flo's hands relating the story. The dramatic hand movements added tension and emotion to the tale. The child was still very confused about the whole thing. With everything she already knew from Charles, Alice pieced the puzzle together and tried to explain it to her, using signs and arm activity.

'The boy had loved you and you had a baby. It was too small and died.' Flo nodded her understanding. 'Why did you put the baby in the river?'

LAMB. DEAD. RIVER. BABY IN BAG DEAD. RIVER.

'You put the baby in your bag and threw it into the river?'

YES

'Why didn't you come home?'

FRIGHTENED.

Alice hugged her daughter tightly and kissed the top of her head as the girl wept in her arms. Why must it take a tragedy like this for mother and daughter to show affection? The love had always been there, what had been lacking was an understanding of one another and openness.

If only Alice had been able to show her a mother's love in infancy, but hugs and kisses had been in a noticeably short measure. There had been no time for displays of affection or moments of maternal fondness. The best gift to give a child is time. But time was precious when trying to care for a sick mother, a hungry family and keeping a drunken father at bay.

Caring for a child's physical needs is not enough, their emotional needs are just as great if not greater. Was it too late for them? Her own tears fell into Flo's soft, clean hair making it shine in the wetness.

Although she knew she would not hear her Alice said softly. 'I named you after a good woman, known for her kind and gentle ways. Florence, I wish I had been able to see your own gentleness. I wish I had taken the time to learn who you are.'

There was a gentle tap at the door and then Charles popped his head into the room.

'I believe my two favourite ladies are in here?' His cheerful grin lightened up the room.

'Please come in, Charles.' Alice strained her neck to look over the top of Flo's head. Now that she had her daughter, she did not wish to let her go.

'I can see that everything is all right in here then.'

'Yes, Charles we are both fine. Thank you for bringing her home to me.' Flo broke away from her mother when she realised his presence and she smiled at him.

'Can she read my lips?' He asked.

'Yes, she reads very well as long as you speak clearly and face her.' Replied Alice. 'We have had quite a long chat, and she has told me everything as she understands it, but you must realise that her understanding of things is limited. I had not told her about certain personal relationships, I suppose I was trying to protect her. Hence the infant.' Charles held out the parcel he had brought for Flo.

Eagerly she tore at the brown paper and revealed her quilted bag. She took a sharp intake of breath when she saw it and flung it away from her shaking her head violently.

'I thought she would be pleased to have it back!' Charles said. Alice tried to get her attention again by gripping her shoulder.

'Flo what is the matter.' Flo's hands and arms flew about as if in a rage. Charles watched them in amazement that Alice was able to interpret the meaning. 'she's saying that she put the baby in the bag and threw it in the river. She cannot understand why you have brought it to her. Are you punishing her for killing the baby? No. Flo. Listen.' She mouthed the words carefully and slowly signed. 'He didn't know. Charles found the bag and thought it was yours. He is sorry.' She turned away from her face and whispered to Charles. 'Tell her you found it.'

'That's right I found it. The man who took you away had it.' He mouthed slowly. Too slowly as people did when they first tried to talk to Flo. It took practice to know just how well she could read lips.

'Bert had it.' said Alice, shocked.

'Yes, I picked it up by the river where I found him. I knew, or I thought it must belong to Flo, so I had it washed and repaired for her.' Flo watched their lips moving with interest.

'It's her bag. I made it from a cape that belonged to my mother. How did Bert get hold of it?'

'He must have dragged it out of the river. I told you that George had found the...' He saw Flo's interest. 'Erm, package but he said nothing about a bag.'

'George would have recognised it if he had. Flo used to carry it everywhere, everyone who knew her knew the bag she carried with her pencils and sketch paper inside.'

'Then I would guess Bert found it first or saw her throw it. He was on the road living rough.' Alice nodded. Her mother had worn the cape until it was threadbare. Bert had grabbed it off her shoulders during his violent drunken outbursts, calling it a tattered old rag.

'Either way he would have recognised the fabric.' She concluded.

'WHO BERT?' Flo was tugging at her mother's sleeve for attention like a petulant child.

'He was the man who took you away.' Alice tried to keep her voice and manner calm so she would not frighten her.

'OLD SMELLY MAN?'

'Yes, Flo.' Charles went to the window and turned his back before speaking again.

'I think we had better discuss this outside.' Alice agreed and motioned that she would follow him then she spoke to Flo again.

'You need rest. Lay down and I will see you in the morning.' She tucked the sheet up around Flo and kissed her gently on the cheek. 'Goodnight darling.'

Flo turned onto her side and closed her eyes, but she knew she would not sleep. They were going to talk about her and what had happened. She was not upset anymore. Her Alice loved her, and she was happy. If only that rotten butler would leave Alice alone, she could have her to herself again. That would be a joyful day for her when she could have Alice to herself.

Back in the kitchen Charles and Alice sat on the settle by the unlit fire trying to make sense of the events. Charles pieced together what they knew.

'If I have gotten this right, Bert found the baby first and recognised the bag. He must have seen Flo throw a bundle into the river and then followed her when he recognised the fabric as you suggested.'

'Why else would he take her? She looks enough like me for him to guess who she was, especially with the bag as a clue.' Her mother's cape was turning out to be fated. First, it had hidden her mother's 'treasure', which had been the means of her escape from poverty and now it had led to Flo's kidnap and the terrible ordeal. The remnants of the cape were back in her room wrapped around the silver spoons. The only mementoes she had of her mother.

'Oh, he knew who she was, he said it was your daughter when he offered her to me.' Charles waited for her reaction, which he knew would be one of horror.

'He did what?' Alice exclaimed although she should not be surprised at anything her father could do. 'Well, he got what he deserved when you hit him and if the blow had been enough to kill him, I'm glad.' She leaned her arms on the table and held her head. 'What a mess this is all turning into. What we should be doing is deciding how to deal with Flo. What am I going to do with her? I can't take her back to the House, after Moll's outburst, and she cannot stay here for much longer. The Coopers are good people, but I can't expect their charity indefinitely.'

'What about taking her to Cissy?' It was the only solution to the problem. The Coopers had been kind, but it was only a small cottage and Mr Cooper had taken to sleeping in the loft with George.

'She doesn't really know Cissy; she was just a child when we left.'

'I'm sure if you took her through Cissy would have her

177

until Flo had recovered.' Alice looked thoughtful. The 'Family' was off on their travels again tomorrow. They were going up to Scotland so she might be able to get leave, but.

'Things are a bit awkward at the House.' She finally said. Charles frowned.

'But why? Surely, they will give you leave, they know Flo is ill.'

'I had words with Mr Evans. He wasn't happy about Moll's outburst. You see there was an understanding that we were to marry.' The look on Charles' face was one of outrage. The Butler was almost old enough to be her father and such a Po-faced stuffed shirt; he was not at all suitable for his Alice. 'He is waiting for an excuse to see me go and this might be all he needs. If I take leave, he might not allow me back. It is in his power to ask me to leave, and he doesn't need to give any reason.'

'So, she will have to stay here until we think of something. Don't worry Alice, something will present itself as the answer.' He had never quite liked this Mr Evans and he would find it hard to believe that Alice had contemplated marriage to such a person. He had come to find her just in time.

TWENTY-ONE

The next morning Flo rose feeling well and full of energy. Everything was good in the world. She and Alice were back together, and they knew that there was a love between them that could not break. Mrs Cooper had cleared away her breakfast things and gone down the lane to see her daughter, leaving the invalid to her own devices.

It felt good to be out in the clean fresh open air. She skipped for a few yards feeling the warm morning air fill her lungs and blow in her hair that flew free of her ribbons. She found herself walking towards the old barn but discovered she was unable to enter. Her heart fluttered uneasily as she stood in the wide doorway. The grass was damp with the dew however she sat down with her back against the weathered wood of the barn door. The wetness seeping into her skirts.

She saw the horse and rider in the distance and recognised them at once. David rode at a walk toward her, dismounting just a few feet from where she sat. Without invitation, he sat down on the wet grass beside her, and they sat in companionable silence for a moment or two.

He took her hand in his and turned to face her.

'I was very worried about you Flo. Please don't ever do that to me again.' He was very sincere, and she felt that.

'SORRY.' He did not know the whole story, but he heard that she was home and that was all that he cared about. This girl had been his friend since he first noticed her hiding in the shrubbery with her coal and amazing talent. He loved her and longed to be able to hold her as lovers should, but he knew that it could never be, so he kept his feelings to himself promising to be her protector forever. The girl by his side looked so forlorn. He put a protective arm around her, and she rested her head on his shoulders. There was no need for words between these two friends.

That is how George saw them when he rounded the wood below the barn. It enraged him to see them embraced like lovers. His anger carried him up the steep slope and without warning, he grabbed the young man dragging him up from the grass and flung him away from Flo.

David composed himself quickly from the abrupt removal from his seat.

'What on earth is wrong with you?' He bellowed at his assailant. Flo had risen from her damp seat and was pulling George away from his target.

'You leave her alone you Bastard! Stay away from her.' George was not usually a violent man he much preferred to step aside from fights and arguments. This was so out of character for the mild-mannered man, girlish tears were rising in the heat of his anger. He aimed a very shaky fist at the young master from the big house but due to Flo's hand on his arm, he missed by inches. David ducked away and held his arm up in defence.

'Stop it. I've never touched her in that way.' His words went unheard. George shook off Flo's hold and dived at David. They were of a similar height, but George was a good stone heavier and a lot fitter because of the heavy farm work. He placed two heavy blows at the younger man's face leaving red marks on his left cheek. David backed away from the angry farmer he would not fight back; he knew he would always lose against such an opponent. He staggered towards the horse grazing a couple of yards away and quickly mounted. From this vantage point, he shouted to Flo.

'I am going away Flo, but I will be back in a few weeks.' He saw her nod her understanding.

'Don't bother,' George shouted back. The horse cantered away leaving Flo punching and kicking at a bemused defender of her virtue. The two dogs who were constantly by his side were barking and joining in the fun that the master seemed to be having. George eventually overpowered her, and she fell to the ground weeping. He stared down confused and disappointed at her behaviour.

After what she had been through, she should be wary of such men trying to take advantage, he was only trying to protect her. He marched away in a sulk he would never understand girls, especially sisters.

Flo wept quietly on the ground. That stupid oaf of a brother had sent off her best friend and she would not see him again for weeks. She sat and dozed by the barn door her mind racing with the events of the past few days. By the time she woke the sun was higher by an hour. With an impulse, she began walking towards the High Fell.

After his conversation with Alice, Charles thought he might be able to persuade Owen Evans to allow her time off. Surely, he could not hold her there under the circumstances. He did not know the man that well, but the butler must think enough of her to see that she needed a break. So, he had a close shave and greased down his hair before saddling his horse and riding off towards the House.

The August heat had not yet risen to its full potential, but it promised to be a real scorcher. The sun had already burnt off the few morning clouds leaving a bright azure blue sky. The stable yard looked deserted, the usual comings and goings had ground to a halt. It was just as it was when he first arrived in what seemed like years ago but in fact, was only a few days. Then there was a search party out looking for Flo; there was no clue as to why they were all missing today. He walked to the kitchen door but before he was it able to knock Moll opened it, she was looking out for him.

She spoke first.

'Oh! Hello Big Fellow.' She was over-friendly, which put Charles on his guard. He knew he should not trust her. 'Everyone is out at the front of the house preparing to go to Scotland with the family. Most of the staff go with them when they go up there. Don't worry though Alice isn't going, nor am I.' She flashed her once enigmatic smile which was now more like a sneer. The lines on her mouth emphasised her thin colourless mouth hardened by years of bitterness.

With a forceful shove, she pushed him away from the doorway. 'Old Po-Face Evans is going though so you'll have Alice all to yourself. It's her you came to see. Of course, it is.' Each time he tried to reply she gave him a little shove in the chest and spoke first. 'I don't think that you should go in there, yet Po-face has been in a funny mood all morning. Go over to the old storeroom behind the stables and I'll fetch her for you. Better still I'll show you where it is.'

She took his arm and dragged him unwillingly towards the stables.

'I would rather wait here, Moll.' He tried to pull his arm away, but her grip was tight on his sleeve. She stopped and turned to him.

'No trust me. It would not be good for Alice if he knew you were here. He knows you are taking her away from him you see. He was going to marry her until you came along. You don't want her to lose her job, do you?' She sounded earnest enough in her argument. It was true that Alice was considering marriage to Owen Evans even if the thought turned his stomach. Moll was right, and he should not be so distrustful of her.

'All right Moll, I'll wait for you to bring her to me but if it is difficult for her to get away, please tell me and I'll call back when they've all gone.' He began to walk with her.

'Oh, they'll all be gone in half an hour or so. Then she'll be free to see you.' They reached the stone outbuilding. It lay a few hundred yards from the stables; built entirely of stone with a huge wooden barn door it housed spare hay for the stables and some old tackle. Charles wandered into the dimness; there was only a small window about five feet from the ground. His eyes became accustomed to the gloom as a sudden pain hammered into his head. The gloom became black as he hit the floor.

* * *

At the front of the house, the remaining servants were waving goodbye to the party leaving for the highlands of Scotland. It had been a habit of the Family to spend the sweltering summer weeks in their highland home.

David had been born in the Scottish Castle, a very imposing name for an inconspicuous, but large building.

The skeleton staff who held the place together during the weeks of the family's absence, trebled when they were in residence.

The maids and kitchen staff had to take turns travelling, Cook was the only member of staff that never went. There was a perfectly good cook available there. There was no need for her to suffer that terrible journey.

As the coaches and flat carts trundled up the driveway the remaining staff wandered away to their duties. Moll took Alice to one side and whispered with mock friendliness.

'Your friend Mr Bingham has been to see you. I told him I would take you to him.'

'Have you left him in the kitchen?'

'I thought it best not to bring him in, he's waiting out the back.' Puzzled at Moll's behaviour Alice lamely followed her out to the back of the house through the kitchen and into the yard. Cook was sound asleep in the armchair, her quiet growl of a snore the only sound in the kitchen.

Once in the yard, Moll pointed to the outbuilding in the distance. Alice walked quickly in front of her and towards the old storehouse with her companion close on her heels. As she entered the gloomy building, she called out his name. A couple of steps into the cool disused store she stumbled over a discarded sack. She looked down at the obstruction and saw Charles lying prone on the floor. There was a trickle of blood running down his temple and into his ear. As she stooped down with a gasp, the huge barn door closed behind her. She heard Moll outside shouting.

'This is what happens when you're bad. You should know that because you two have been bad.' Alice could hear Moll walking up and down past the shuttered door. 'I hope it's not too dark in there. It was dark when I was bad. Did you know that I was bad? Of course, you did, you helped me to be bad didn't you Charlie boy?' Charles was regaining consciousness, he groaned as Alice tried to wipe the blood from his bruised head. She shushed and quietened him like a hurt child.

Moll went quiet, which worried Alice. The best thing that she could hope for was that she had grown bored with her taunting and left them locked in. But Moll continued with her taunts.

'Go on, shout! I want to hear you shout.' Alice did not comply. Moll paced up and down in front of the barn door. 'I used to sing to myself.' She began to sing. 'BAH Black sheep' but stumbled over the words. 'I was supposed to sing hymns, but I tore up the book my dad threw at me. Here's one you'll like.' She sang her rendition of 'Ring o ring of roses.' Alice tried to sit Charles up, but his body was limp and heavy. There was silence. Moll had stopped singing. Had she gone away?

The first wave of smoke drifted over the top of the musty pile of hay and Alice panicked. The flickering flames grew rapidly and licked hungrily at the dry contents of the barn. She desperately heaved at the inanimate body at her feet, inching him away from the fire and towards the door. Her hand beat against the door, and she screamed for help, would anyone hear her screams or see the smoke? The heavy black smoke filled her lungs slowly choking her screams.

'Oh, God.' She screamed. 'Why is this happening?' She held him close, wiping the sweat from his brow. He murmured her name. 'Don't worry my love we will get out of this. We must.

We were meant to be together Charles but not to die like this. Someone will see the smoke and get us out, I'm sure.' She turned and beat her feet against the heavy doors and shouted for help.

The House looked peaceful from the hillside. Flo hoped that she would see David before he left. She needed to apologise for her brother's shameful behaviour. Her recent misfortune had left her weak making it necessary for her to rest often. Halfway down the gentle hillside, she stopped to take a breath. She was nearing the house from the rear and could see the stables and outbuildings. When Alice appeared with Moll, Flo waved her arms at the two women who did not see the distant figure.

Once more she walked carefully down the slope. Why had Moll put the bar across the door with Alice still inside? Moll was shouting something animatedly at the building waving her arms about. She did not see the lantern Moll threw into the window and amongst the hay, but her keen sense of smell soon noticed the smoke.

Alice was in there; she had to get her out. If only her legs would move faster but she hurt so much. Her arms and stomach felt like lead dragging her down. Running, crawling, slipping and sliding on the grassy slope she reached the outbuilding in what seemed like hours. Tears of frustration stung her eyes.

Alice weakly cried out, the sound of her coughing punctuating the shouts for help. Flo felt the beat on the door, Alice was in there, but she could not get it open, the door barred tight Flo pushed and pushed but the heavy oak beam would not budge.

Alice hammered with her fist and then her feet against the door desperate to escape the searing heat. Her assault on the door against Flo's struggles somehow loosened the bar and with a final effort from the girl on the outside the heavy bar fell to the ground with a thud. The huge door flew open with the weight of Alice against it. Her face burned red with the heat from the fire and her breath came in heavy gasps Alice crawled out of the blazing building. Flo dashed forward, the heat billowing out took her breath. She grabbed at her mother's blackened blouse pulling her away from the encroaching flames. Alice would not let go of Charles; she was frantically trying to pull him outside with her.

With Flo to help the two women dragged him clear of the building. As the door opened a plume of black choking smoke billowed out and aimed for the fresh blue sky. Two figures came running at the sight.

Old Tom and young Pete from the stables rounded the comer just in time to see young Flo and the assistant cook pulling the big fellow from the burning building. Alice cradled Charles's bruised and blackened head.

'We are safe Geordie, now you must promise not to upset me like that again.' Her tears mingled with the soot on his face and traced down his temple. She knew now that she loved him and had always done. Since she had left that hovel by the docks her life had been safe but lacking in vitality. The day-to-day struggle of keeping body and soul together had blinded her to the one spark in her miserable life. Her daily battles with the huge dock man. He was back, Flo was safe, and now they were not to perish on the whim of a mad woman.

TWENTY-TWO

His head still ached from the blow although the wound was only a minor cut. Alice had tended the wound and stemmed the blood; she washed the dried blood from his hair and the sooty marks from his face with tenderness. Cook made cups of tea for everyone and berated Moll for her actions.

'She's gone too far this time. Waltzed in here like nothing was wrong and said she was going to set the fires in the library. That's when I knew she was off her tree. She's never been right since she came back. Of course, you wouldn't remember it was before your time here Alice.' She clattered the teacups as she talked. 'I've sent her upstairs to her room. Young Polly is watching her.'

'I think she needs help Cook,' Alice still did not blame the poor demented woman for her wicked actions.

'You know that she set alight to that place on purpose, don't you?' Cook said. 'She was like this once before when she first came back after her illness. One of the outside staff brought his wife and new baby to visit. To show them off, as people do. Lovely baby he was. He had lots of black hair, all shiny and curly and the most angelic smile. Moll took to the child all lovey-dovely, cooing and such. She only went and cut the little baby's hair off in great chunks. I remember the poor child's mother was beside herself.'

'She didn't hurt the boy, though, did she?' The story

shocked Alice but could not believe Moll was anything but as disturbed as her own mother had been. It was different for Moll in some ways, but she was hurting inside.

'No, she didn't but she might have if we hadn't found her. She was singing lullabies to the child as she chopped at his hair. We watched her every moment after that, but she still sang to herself, and I heard her talking to the walls once.' The old lady had never had to deal with mental illness or depression. All her life she had been happy. Happy in her blissful childhood with wonderful parents then happy in service doing what she loved, cooking for the huge staff at High Fell and caring for her husband.

His death was the only sadness she had ever known, but he went peacefully and left her memories to cherish. She had never had a child and had never known the love a mother has for her baby. Of course, she thought she understood, but the truth was that she never could.

Flo lay curled up on the floor sound asleep, exhausted by her earlier efforts. Charles still felt drowsy and there was a pounding like a dozen carthorses' hooves in his head. Alice's pain was deep in her chest where she had inhaled the acrid smoke but also in her heart worried for Moll.

* * *

Moll had slept for a while; she lay quiet on the bed eyes closed and her breathing shallow. Polly dozed while her charge was quiet, the key to the door nestled safely in her pocket. The captive opened one eye and looked across at her sleeping gaoler. 'Mother must be losing her mind if she thinks this slip of a girl could keep me locked up.' Moll's mind had gone back years; back to the day when her parents had first taken her sanity.

Slowly and stealthily, she rose from the wooden bed. She took the bundle of clothes from the chair and cradled it gently.

'Shush there.' She whispered to the imaginary baby.

'Mammy will look after you.' She looked over to the sleeping girl careful not to wake her. The window was easy to open but the climb to the top of the roof proved more challenging for a woman in a long nightgown and bare feet.

Young Polly woke with a start, she had not meant to sleep but she was so tired. It took her a moment to realise where she was and why. The empty bed confused her for a split second but suddenly, on seeing the window open, realised her charge was on the roof. She stuck her head as far out of the window as she dared. Moll was nowhere in sight, but she heard her singing. Like a frightened rabbit, Polly ran down the four flights of stairs and breathlessly flew into the kitchen. She was pointing upwards and swallowing hard to catch her breath.

'She's on the roof.' These were the only words she could find. There was no need for further explanations. Cook pulled her bulky frame out of the chair with more speed than she had ever managed in her whole life. Befuddled and still light-headed, Charles followed her out into the yard. The stable boys and the gardener joined the group watching the woman dancing on the roof.

Balancing on the apex she was singing at the top of her voice and rocking a white bundle like a baby.

Alice had instead run up the stairs with the young kitchen maid in her wake. As she entered the empty attic bedroom, she heard the singing.

'Rock a bye baby on the treetop,
When the wind blows the cradle will rock.
When the bough breaks the cradle will fall,
Down will come baby cradle and all.
La la la la lah'

Moll was starting on another verse of the lullaby and the audience down below saw her turn to walk along the roof's apex.

'Rock a bye baby on the treetop, when the wind blows the cradle will rock.' She slipped and landed on the hard roof tiles banging her bottom and back, but she would not leave go of

189

the 'baby' to save herself. Her nightgown ripped and tore as she tumbled her way down the slate roof. She was still holding the bundle tightly to her breast as she hit the hard-stone ground four floors below.

The doctor left minutes after his arrival; there was nothing he could do. He found it hard to believe that she had been cleaning the window when she fell, but all the staff agreed that she was hanging too far out onto the sill. The doctor sedated young Polly with laudanum, she was in such a state.

Alice quietly packed her few belongings. She could not stay; it would be far too distressful. Moll's parents had taken their only daughter's body away; they had seemed surprisingly unaffected by her death. They had acted so cold and unemotional, not even asking how the accident had happened.

After the fire and death of Moll, Alice decided to take Flo to live with Cissy. While the family were away it seemed the best time to go. Her possessions were few and soon packed away into an old pillowcase. The small wooden box she kept under her bed held her treasures. She took a private moment to look through the box. Flo's pictures, two small finely embroidered handkerchiefs sent to her from Cissy a couple of Christmases ago and the perfect cotton gloves she gave her for her birthday last year. She kept her savings in there, quite a bit put by now as she did not spend her wages.

Nestled in the bottom sat the remains of her mother's cape. Flo's sketch bag had taken the fabric but wrapped in the remnants were four small insignificant silver spoons. The cloth and the spoons were all that remained of her mother. She laid the fabric on her lap and unwrapped it carefully. The small spoons had gone and in their resting place, there was a letter addressed to her in Owen's fine handwriting. She tore it open, curious and puzzled she read.

My dearest Alice,
Please do not think badly of me when you find that your

treasure has gone. Moll told me what you had hidden, and my curiosity got the better of me. When you find this note, please do not approach me but rest assured that I have your best interests at heart in taking the spoons.

I do not wish to know how you came to have four teaspoons belonging to The Marsden Family. It is enough to say that they went missing some time ago, along with the rest of the family silver. I have put them in a safe place and when the opportunity arises, I will introduce them back to the correct place.

I am doing this sweet Alice to save you from the terrible trouble that could befall you if Moll were to tell anyone else, and because I think so very highly of you.

I can see that you are not meant for me, but my dear it will be so extremely hard to keep my feelings hidden.

Please forgive me and remember that I will remain your friend.

> *Your dearest Friend*
> *Owen*

So, he did love her or respect her enough to protect her from Moll's vicious tongue. Sadness fell over her, she would never see her mother's treasure again for she could never approach Owen and ask him to return the spoons. He had recognised them as the family silver and he would feel honour bound to return them to their rightful owner, no matter what she said.

Fingering the raised threads of the fabric she pictured her poor mother in the kitchen rocking backwards and forwards on the rickety chair. How things had changed since that fateful moment when Alice had held her dying mother in her arms. Her father had stood over the tableau with terror written deep in his soul. The child Flo played happily with the contents of the shopping bag oblivious to the tragedy that had just occurred.

She had never seen her father again but now she knew he was dead and may have died by the hand of the man who had shadowed her life. The man she had run away from because she was afraid of turning into her mother.

EPILOGUE

The view from the window was changing rapidly. Gone were the old grey stoned cottages. Stacked high on one side of the site were the huge cornerstones, and another pile consisted of the smaller reusable blocks and the best of the bricks. The rubbish left by the travellers and vagrants, who had been the only tenants for five years, kindled the fires that had been set to rid the place of the damp worm-ridden wood. It gladdened her to watch the miserable dwellings getting demolished.

When Charles had told her that the row of cottages belonged to her, she said not to tease, but he was telling her the truth. With the money he had earned in America the first thing he had done on his return was to buy the whole row in her name. Whether she married him or not, they were hers to do with as she pleased.

They had talked about the future and of the past, like old friends who needed to catch up on old times. She knew so much about him she now regretted the years that they had missed. Charles Bingham now had a position of authority on the dockside. He knew all the tricks and swindles that could be pulled and as a result, the men respected him.

As the demolition men worked down below, she watched with immense pleasure.

The inspiration for the school sat over by the desk her

head buried in another book. Flo recovered well from her experience and began to blossom once again. Her cheeks had colour and her beautiful dark wavy hair was again shining with vitality. If Alice had enjoyed fresh air and freedom to run when she was a child, she would have been the image of Flo.

On reflection, Flo had turned out well. Alice knew now that if she had left her in York with Mrs Samuelson Flo would have become a very precocious child, protected and mollycoddled by the woman. She needed to run, learn who she was and make her own mistakes. She did not need protection from the world or from her disability. Together Alice and Flo had taught each other what they needed. The time spent with Cissy chatting, sewing and making plans had brought the three 'sisters' together.

The noisy arrival of her hostess broke her thoughts.

'What's happening Alice?' She rushed to her sister's side and looked out of the window. 'The speed at which the men are working the place will be cleared before the end of the week, then the building will begin.' She hugged Cissy to her in a sisterly fashion and her sister reacted with a dig in the older girl's ribs.

'Who would have thought that two snotty-nosed urchins like us would own the street? I cannot believe it myself. Come on down now your dress is ready for a fitting.' Flo designed her mother's wedding dress and Cissy was, of course, stitching it.

Joe would give her away at the ceremony and Eddie, George and the Coopers would be attending.

She was so happy that she could burst. Once the house and school were up and running and she was helping deaf children to read, write and sign, her life would be complete.

ABOUT THE AUTHOR

L.m.fewtrell

I was born in 1952 in Middlesbrough, the fourth child in a family of six. My head was stuck in a book as soon as I could read. My working life has been varied, nursing, shop assistant and dental receptionist are among the many roles I took. Writing short stories for my own pleasure whenever I could. I wrote my first book 'When the bough breaks' in about 1998, and a few close friends and family read it before it went into the attic with all the short stories. With the growth of the computer age, I wrote blogs about my experiences with the public and my trips abroad, all stored neatly away in the magic that is the cloud. When I met another keen amateur writer, and we shared our ideas, she encouraged me to get published. Now I am retired I hope to find the time to get all my stories down and hopefully printed. Thank you for reading my first novel. If you have enjoyed my story, please leave feedback on Amazon.

BOOKS BY THIS AUTHOR

Down In The Valley

Their first family holiday turns into a nightmare when, on an innocent, early morning ride to the bakery leaves Paul desperately searching for his wife. She has no memory of her life before or the attack which left her fighting for life in a deserted valley

The Adventures Of Edith And Edna

Two old friends finding their way through old age together, with laughter along the way

Printed by Amazon Italia Logistica S.r.l.
Torrazza Piemonte (TO), Italy

41326770R00117